WITHIN A NAME

ROBERT FISHER

BIOGRAPHY

Robert Fisher has lived in Hiroshima, Japan, with his wife and five-year-old son since 2015, where he occasionally teaches English, writes, and pretends to learn Japanese. Before that, he lived in Vancouver, Canada, where he worked in the beer industry and mostly just cavorted about, getting into trouble and eating Thai food. He placed fourth in The *Vancouver Courier*'s literary contest with his short story "The Gift," which appeared in that paper on February 20, 2009. His science-fiction novella *The God Machine* was published by Blue Cubicle Press in 2011, and *The Kalis Experiments,* the first book in the *Tides Trilogy,* was released by Next Chapter in August, 2019.

ACKNOWLEDGMENTS

Thank you, Tomomi, for everything (literally). Thank you Beckett, for knowing when I needed a break. You shan't ever be forgotten.

Thanks to the 3 Day Novel Contest, for forcing me to write the first draft of this book over one weekend.

CHAPTER ONE

Ranat Totz's worn shoe made a sodden, squishy noise when he poked the corpse with his toe. The sound was barely audible over the soft patter of the drizzle.

He glanced around. Somewhere, beyond the low rough slate of clouds, the sun edged its way over the horizon. People already thronged the narrow street behind him. This early in the morning, it was traders and merchants with their servants and hangers-on in tow, bustling down Grace's Walk, eyes on the wagons hauling bolts of cloth or lumber or smoked fish, or whatever else could be sold in the markets. Minds on wealth, their accumulation of it, or their lack of it. Spitting, coughing camels pulled the carts, snipping and grunting at anyone who stumbled too near. Beggars from the Lip weaved between the knots of merchants, their pleas riding across the din and rattle of the street: "Tin? Have a Tin? A Three-Side? A disk? Even a ball? One copper ball? A draw from your cask, there?"

The thrum of it was familiar music to the old ears of Ranat, but the last question, which carried to him before the bray of a disgruntled camel cut the voice off, made his mouth water. Not that he'd ever resort to begging traders. They weren't known to part with their booze or tin. Still, he could use a drink.

He took a furtive glance around again and ran a long, weathered finger down his jawline, felt the steel wire tangle of his short white beard. A tremor, the first of the day, shuddered through his fingers, taking on a life of its own as it fluttered down his arm. Yeah. A drink would be good.

No one was paying attention to Ranat, where he hovered on the edge of the darkness cast between two crooked windowless tenements, and no one but he had seen the corpse so far, obscured by a moth-eaten sack of stiff, coarse cloth that had been thrown over the body, but had failed to completely cover it.

He crouched by the figure and tugged off the ragged shroud of burlap to get a better look. The alley was cobbled here, but close to the Lip and coated in a fingers-width of slick black mud, grasping at anything that sunk into it. A few paces further in, a soft low belch rumbled from the ground. A brass-release valve rigged to the Tidal Works began to sigh thick white steam. The warm cloud churned over Ranat for a moment before a subtle shift in the air, unseen and unfelt, funneled it upward in a slow tornado, where it vanished in the eternal grey ceiling that hung above the city of Fom.

It was a man. Face down. Black hair shot with a few dashes of silver. Well off. Some Church official, though what he'd been doing out here on the edge of the Lip before dawn was an interesting question.

Ranat took a deep breath, held it, let it go. Forced his hands to stop shaking. Then, he went to work. The coat was nice—heavy, light grey leather dusted with a coating of fine white hair. He worked it over the dead man's shoulders and tried it on, brushing without success at the mud caked onto the front of it. It fit. A little big, but Ranat wasn't going to complain about that. The boots were better than the ones he was wearing now, too, but way too big. Still, he pulled them off and bundled them in the damp wad of burlap that had hidden the corpse. He knew a guy by the arena that would pay cash for the leather if he couldn't find another taker for them.

He suppressed a shudder as he flipped the body over, and the mud made a soft, sucking sound as it clung to the man's chest and thighs and face. The body was pudgy, but pasty mud masked all other features, except the color of his hair. *Just another body*, he told himself. No reason it should be any different

3

than the ones he normally picked from, except that this one wasn't already buried.

The man's shirt was black with old blood, where it wasn't crusted in mud. There was a tear just below the heart, as long as Ranat's thumb. He shuddered again, looking down at the stains on his new coat. Just mud stains, he told himself, peering at them, not too close, in the shadows of the alley. Just mud.

The dull clatter of tin as he'd rolled the body had made him pause, and now he saw what caused it: a heavy-looking, once fine belt pouch pregnant with coins. He couldn't have been laying here for more than a few hours then, even this early in the morning. Someone would have taken the cash. Shit, Ranat thought. One hour in this part of town was stretching it. More like twenty minutes. He felt panic rise in his stomach, sure someone must be watching him, and he rose to check the street again, but amid the teeming mass of people, he was still alone.

Coin. He'd got lucky. The pouch bulged as he fondled the clasp that attached it to the dead man's belt. Not just tin balls and disks, but Three-Sides. Ranat would be able to drink for a month. Maybe more, if he paced himself and stuck to glogg.

His long fingers hesitated over the belt buckle he was trying to unlatch as his gaze fell on it for the first time. He sucked in a little whistle of breath through the gap made by his two missing upper-front teeth. Even through the greasy, briny mud, he could tell the buckle was precious. Crystals—or were they diamonds?—peeked through the seeping gaps of black ooze where Ranat's fumbling fingers had scraped it clean. Other gemstones, green and yellow, formed the angular, stylized shape of a phoenix, with a single square ruby serving as the bird's eye. All of it set into the metal of the buckle itself. And not just copper or bronze. The thing held the grey, dull weight of iron.

Ranat finished tugging the belt loose and bundled it with the boots. He patted down the rest of the body. In a narrow pocket on the inner thigh, he found a letter, chunks of a broken seal of black wax still attached to it. One edge of it was stained dark and ruddy with blood. His heart lurched with excitement, but he resisted the urge to read it. Better to wait until he was out of the rain. Better to get away from this damn corpse before someone saw him standing over it and got the wrong idea.

He took a few steps towards Grace's Walk, paused, and went back to the alley. He crouched down, one last time, this time to wipe the mud on the dead man's face with a handful of dripping rags heaped by a nearby doorway. The sheer wealth of the dead man was astounding, more so for where he'd ended up in the end, and Ranat half expected to recognize the soft round features, but wiped clean there was nothing familiar in the face.

"Well," he said to himself. "I've got to get the hell out of here."

He stepped onto Grace's Walk again and crossed to the unnamed streets beyond, still doing his best to pretend the uneven, dark stains on the lapels of his new coat were from the mud. He heaved the sack with the boots and belt over his shoulder, and every few steps double-checked to make sure the pouch of tin was still secure under his threadbare linen shirt. He'd need to unload the boots and the buckle soon, if for no other reason than he didn't want to carry them around, but first, he needed a drink.

———

Noble sir,

Please consider this an invitation to discuss the new situation in a more informal capacity. While you will find me in reluctant accord regarding most details, there are a few points I would like you to consider.

I have reserved a booth at The Crow's Marquis for the balance of the day, where I hope you will grace me with your wisdom.

With the utmost respect,

Your servant in Grace

Ranat drained his glass and set it among the empty ones lining the edge of the warped table, a leaning construction of driftwood and ancient shattered pallets, fitted together and tossed with apparent randomness, along with other similar bits of furniture, into the basement that everyone referred to as "the bar."

He took a long pull from the next glass—the eighth on the table and the last one to be emptied—and examined what remained of the wax seal, thankful the quiver in his hands was gone.

Black wax. An image of a tree, a crescent moon hanging over it, some sort of creature seated among the stylized roots. Enough of it had crumbled away to keep what sort of animal it was—other than one with antlers or horns—a mystery.

Ranat read the letter again, savoring the shapes of the words as they panned across his eyes. He didn't understand what it was telling him. He'd never heard of The Crow's Marquis. Still, it was a more interesting read than the usual manifests and shipping lists that he ended up collecting most of the time.

The note explained a few things, though. Whoever the corpse had been, he'd been up to something. A Church official, maybe, trying to do some business on the side. Something shady. Something that had gone south in a hurry, and left the man a crumpled body in an anonymous alley in Fom, stabbed through the heart.

"Should have minded his own goddamn business," Ranat muttered, glancing over the paper one more time before folding it back up and slipping it into the pocket of his new coat.

"What was that? Shit, Ranat, I guess that's not your blood, or you'd be passed out with seven and a half beers in you."

He looked toward the voice. He'd been focused on the letter for longer than he'd thought. The bar had filled from the smattering of vagabonds that had been there when he'd first arrived, the sawdust floor almost hidden through the mass of legs, and the stone walls bled condensation from a hundred alcohol-infused breaths. Light seeping around the front door, loose and crooked in its frame, was a watery yellow from glow lamps instead of the watery grey of daylight. Somewhere, beyond the gritty overcast, the sun had set.

The speaker was a pocked, wiry woman with sharp, clear eyes and a knotted ponytail of sandy hair that looked like she'd tied back weeks ago and ignored ever since. Her face was craggy and pitted, like an old woman drained of her beauty, though Ranat knew she wasn't half his age. Life in the tunnels of the Lip was cruel even to those it was kind to.

"It's not blood, Gessa. It's mud." Ranat gestured the chair opposite him, where his empty glasses cluttered the table.

She shook her head. "Got no tin for beer tonight. Surprised you do." She glanced at the empty glasses.

8

"Not rum or glogg, neither, but beer at that." She paused. "Eight of them. So far."

Ranat shrugged. "Made a find. You want something, it's on me, for once." He shot her a grin, showing off his missing teeth. "Don't expect that offer again anytime soon, either. If I were you, I'd take it."

"A *find*? Who's tomb you dig up now? The former Grace? The goddamn Arch Bishop himself?" But as she spoke, she pulled out the chair, frowned as it wobbled under her, and pushed the empty glasses into the middle of the table.

"No tomb, this time," Ranat said. "Though he wasn't any less dead for the lack of one."

He waved over the waiter, a boy nine or ten, with a vicious rough scar that traversed his shaved head from his right eyebrow to the nape of his neck. "Five more beers. And another one for my friend." He reached into the coat and pulled out a triangular coin, a little smaller than the palm of his hand, stamped with the relief of a dour old man on one side and a stylized sun-and-crescent moon on the other. "And keep it coming," he added as he flipped the coin towards the boy, who nodded and disappeared into the milling throng towards the bar.

Gessa's eyes were wide. "A Three-Side? You *did* make a find, didn't you?"

Ranat scratched his tortured beard and smiled. "Told you. Looks like some poor sot from the estates got into something he couldn't handle. You ask me, they should stay behind their gates where they can feel superior and safe, like. It's dangerous in the city. You hear anything about it yet?"

"You mean about someone important turning up dead?" She shrugged. "No. Not yet, anyway. You know who he was?"

"Nah. Found some boots, though. Too big for me. And a coat. Oh, yeah. And this." He reached under the table into the sack and rummaged through the bottom until his fingers closed around the muddy belt. He pulled it out and draped it across the empty glasses.

Gessa's eyes grew even wider. Her expression was almost comical. Two giant eyes like white-and-blue plates on a narrow rack of a face, dishes set out to dry. "Damn," she said under her breath as she picked up the buckle and felt the weight of it. "Iron?"

"Seems like. Not to mention the stones. Recognize the work?"

"Nah," she said with a shake of her head. "Someone from the Church, though. No one else can afford this. Well, maybe one of the merchants. Where you find the body if he wasn't already tombed up the way you like 'em?"

Ranat scowled, but ignored the jab. "Just yonder. A few streets from the Lip. Heaped in an alley."

Gessa nodded. "Guess he was up to no good, then. Still, what an idiot. Gonna do business on the

Lip, at least dress the part. Come slumming dressed like that, someone'll shank you."

He plucked the belt out of Gessa's hands just as the boy returned with another tray of lagers and struggled to find room for them on the already cluttered table.

Ranat spoke around the boy's fumbling arms. "Yeah, that's what I thought, but he didn't get shanked for his money. Whoever killed him, they just wanted him dead. That's weird, too. If you're gonna murder someone like that, might as well at least make it *look* like a mugging."

"You know where you're gonna unload?" Gessa asked, ignoring the boy, who'd gathered all the empty glasses onto his tray and was now waiting for a break in the crowd to take them back to the kitchen.

"Meh. The boots I think I can take to Han. Even if he doesn't want them, he still owes me for the time I pulled half his inventory out of that fire. Not sure about the belt. Don't know anyone who has the kind of tin lying around to pay up front for something like that, and damn if I'm gonna take less than it's worth. Shit, even without the stones, the iron is worth as much as the sack of cash the poor bastard had on him."

Gessa chewed her lip in silence for a minute. "I know a guy, maybe."

"Some smuggler on the Lip?"

"Nah. He's legit. Pays his Salvation Taxes and everything."

Ranat scowled. "Then why would he deal with me?"

"He knows he can pay you less than that thing is worth, and you'll still walk away happy because it's more than you'll get anywhere else."

"Business first, faith second, eh?" he asked, tone wry.

Gessa shrugged. "Isn't that always how it works?"

"So, I guess you'll be wanting a cut, then, if you tell me where this guy is."

She smiled, revealing teeth the same color as the sawdust floor. "Thirty percent?"

"Ha!"

"Fine then. Don't need to be like that. How about fifteen?"

Ranat laughed, genuine this time. "Shit, woman. I'll make it ten, and throw in a lesson or two on haggling since you seem to be so bad at it."

Gessa frowned, but managed to make the expression friendly. "Fine. Ten. But you owe me."

His smile didn't fade. "What do you mean? I already bought you a beer."

———

It was late when they left the nameless bar, cold enough outside to condense the constant drizzle into a light rain.

"I suppose this mystery merchant of yours doesn't keep night hours," Ranat murmured, turning up his collar against the chill.

"Nah," she said, and looked as if she might add something else, but fell silent.

"Well," Ranat said after a moment. "No use standing in the rain. My place ain't far from here, you know." He gave her a look.

She smiled a little. "Yeah. I know. Let's go."

They made their way through the narrow, winding streets of Fom. After a block, two- and three-story buildings of limestone and narrow cobbled streets gave way to single-story shanties of driftwood and even narrower alleys of mud. Here and there, hidden valves to the Tidal Works opened with soft clicks, and excess steam whistled from vents and copper pipes jutting from the bases of the walls. These gave out, too, when they crossed into the Lip, and guttering torches and the greasy, faint light of oil lanterns replaced the yellow glow lamps.

The Lip was what everyone called the northwestern quadrant of Fom—a dense collection of shacks and lean-tos massed along the cliffs and riding the rotting platforms that lined the limestone face, down to the high-tide line and thrashing waves. The bulk of the Lip was under their feet now, in the warren of tunnels, caverns, quarries, and tombs carved out of the rock that, elsewhere in Fom, were filled with the machines of the Tidal Works that powered the city.

Gessa was a native of The Lip, born and raised, and Ranat knew she was more than capable of navigating the three-dimensional maze that lay below them. He suspected that, like language, it took a childhood knowledge to become fluent. He'd come here fifty years ago and still dreaded descending into the tunnels without a guide.

Ranat's home was on the surface, in the basement of a squat single-story tenement close enough to hear the constant churning of the sea. A stack of moldering wooden beams that seemed to serve no other purpose concealed the entrance to his single room, the door held closed by a simple ceramic lock.

He entered first and made Gessa wait outside while he tiptoed through the stacks of books, letters, and scraps of paper to the oil lamp mounted on the wall, which he lit with a flint hanging next to it on a bit of twine. The high pane-less windows along the ceiling, only a hand's width thick, didn't let in any real light, even during the day, and draped with heavy, mildewed, camel-hair blankets to keep out some of the damp.

Gessa hovered in the doorway, looking around the room in the faint, flickering light. Floor and walls carved from limestone, cut from the bedrock Fom hunkered on. The ceiling was wood, brown and unfinished, warped from relentless moisture. Naked support beams sprouted from the walls and shouldered the load of the sinking floor above.

In one corner, beneath the lamp, a wad of blankets and rags denoted Ranat's bed. Makeshift shelves of driftwood and brick lined the rest of the room, crammed with old books, letters, and stacks of paper. More books and documents lay heaped about the room. Despite the randomness, she suspected there was an organization to the place that made perfect sense in the mind of Ranat Totz.

"In or out," he stated. "I want to close the door."

Gessa stepped in and shut the door behind her. "I see you haven't changed things much since last time I was here," she quipped, looking around for a place to sit. Her eyes rested on a lopsided stool, and she moved the stack of paper that occupied it before sitting down, resting the pile among the others scattered across the floor.

"What's there to change?" He removed the letter he'd found on the body from his coat, took another glance at it, and filed it on one of the shelves.

"Why you have all this stuff, anyway? Shit, can you even read?"

Ranat sat down onto his pile of rags with a groan. "Didn't you ask me that last time you were here?"

"Yeah."

"And what did I say?"

"You said it was a story for another day."

He grumbled with laughter. "Did I? That's a shit answer. Sounds like something I'd say, though."

Gessa didn't bother responding.

"So," Ranat continued. "You want to know, or what? And to answer your question, yeah, I can read."

"Raised in a temple, were you?"

He shot her a glance, but he could tell she was being sincere. "Fair enough question, I suppose. No, I wasn't a temple boy. Grew up on a vineyard."

"Your parents were vintners?"

"Pah! That's a good one. You think I'd live like this? No. Indentured servants. I'd still be there if I hadn't run away. Be there or dead."

"Didn't that just grow your parents' debt, their kid leaving like that?"

Ranat shrugged, looked away from her, focused on nothing. "I was young." His voice was soft.

Gessa cleared her throat and gestured around. "So, how does that explain all this?"

He looked back at her. "I was—hell, I don't know —nine, maybe. Ten. Realized I couldn't fathom picking grapes for the rest of my life. Had this idea to teach myself to read, so I started stealing books from the wine master. Whatever I could get my hands on. Manifests, accounting stuff. Some Church scriptures. Law. Didn't matter. The words were what fascinated me. That those scratches on the page all meant something, and when I put them all together, they meant something else. I couldn't get over it. Think I taught myself how to read through sheer force of will. I needed to know how all those symbols worked together.

"It came easy enough after a while. Eavesdropping on conversations between the master and his bookkeepers helped me get over bumps. After I left and came to the city, I discovered there were other languages out there. N'naradin I'd mastered on the vineyard. Now, I had Skald, Valez. Other puzzles to figure out." He trailed off, looked around his home. "I guess it stuck."

"You can read Skald and Valez, too?" Her voice was incredulous.

Ranat chuckled, but the sound was sad. "Nah, that was my plan, though. Then I found the bottle. Kind of lost my motivation after that."

"And the grave-robbing?" Gessa asked.

Ranat winced but, again, detected no malice or disgust in her voice. Just curiosity. Even so, he couldn't bring himself to meet her gaze. "Burials are public domain," he stated as if that settled things. "Easy enough to find where they inter high-ups, if you can read."

"That doesn't answer the question."

He sighed, looking at her again. She doesn't look that old, he thought. He wondered how he'd gotten the impression that she was. "Doesn't it? Well, life is hard for a kid new to the city. Whether or not he can read. I was too proud to beg like those poor bastards on the Grace's Walk. Too good to steal."

"You steal from the dead." Once again, no malice rode her voice. It was just an observation. She was oblivious to how it might cut.

It was an argument he'd won within himself long ago, in any case. "Can't steal from those that need nothing, Gessa."

She didn't say anything to that.

He studied her. It was her turn to avoid his gaze, and her eyes wandered the room, looking at everything that wasn't him. No, he thought. Not old by a long shot. Just... weathered. Like he could complain about that.

"Anyway, you can spend the night here. If you want."

For an answer, she crossed the room toward him and turned down the lamp.

CHAPTER TWO

His pounding head woke him. He tried to open his eyes, found them too crusted with sleep, rubbed them, and tried again. They peeled back to reveal cracked, harsh light bleeding in from around the camelhair curtains. Even in the basement's twilight, fire burned through his eyes to the back of his head. He groaned and sat up. Hammers struck into his skull.

He closed his eyes, and after a few minutes, tried again. Better this time. His room was blurry, but less washed out than it had been before.

Gessa was gone. He swallowed his disappointment at that. The one other time she'd spent the night, she'd pulled the same thing. He realized he'd been hoping that it would be different, now, after he'd opened up like that. Still, what did he expect? He was an old man with missing teeth and a damn grave robber to boot. Should be glad she spent the night in the first place.

And she'd come through on her side of the bargain, he saw as rose, unsteady. On the stool where she'd sat the night before was a scrap of paper. She'd drawn on the back of one of his letters—a page from a twelve-year-old shipping manifest from a boat called the *Immortal*, he noted with a scowl. A scratched-out map of the part of Fom around Wise Hall, the cathedral itself marked with a lopsided sketch of a sun-and-crescent moon, and a spot a block to the north marked with a little "x" that he presumed was the hawker.

Well, he'd see her again when she came around to get paid, anyway.

He sighed. Even with Wise Hall marked for reference, it would take forever to find the guy he was looking for. He grimaced at the chicken scratches of the map. He didn't even know the hawker's name. Ranat hoped his would be the only merchant on the block. He didn't savor the consequences of asking the wrong person to buy a belt looted from a dead man.

He rummaged through the room, looking for clothes that didn't stink of sweat and booze and, failing that, donned the same ragged linen shirt and tatty pants he'd worn the night before. At least his coat was nice, except for the stains.

———

The hawker was easier to find than Ranat had expected. Gessa's map had been faithful to the twist of Fom's streets, and the hawker's place was indeed the only store of its kind, squeezed between a row of accounting offices and law firms.

The clouds had been high when he'd left his home late that morning; he'd almost dared hope for a rare glimpse of the sun to boil off the rest of his hangover but, as he walked, the overcast had lowered again until the sky seemed to brush the tops of the copper domes that marked the neighborhoods around Wise Hall. Rain pattered the streets, which were well-groomed here, clean of mud. Simple copper vents that blasted steam in other parts of Fom were stylized here into the faces of cherubs and demons, the mist blasting from their mouths and noses before vanishing in the chilly, foggy air. Citizens in this quarter were clean-cut and gave sidelong looks at Ranat as he half-staggered along, courtesy of the hangover.

The ink on Gessa's map began to run in the rain, and he needed to stop in doorways every few blocks to peer at it, trying to make out the shape of the streets.

But this must be the place. A broad, worn stairway, made from the same melting limestone most of the city was built from, led up three small steps to a wide door. Both steps and door squatted beneath a wide awning, clogged with clothes on hangers and shelves crammed with pottery. Within was more of the same and, behind the long counter, thick logs lined the wall with bronze and ceramic swords, axes, and knives lodged into it without obvious organization.

Ranat studied the map again, told himself he was just stalling, and approached the counter.

The man that greeted him with a nod was young despite his bald head, which he'd attempted to disguise with a few wisps of black hair tugged over from the side. He wasn't quite fat, but "portly" didn't do him justice, either.

Ranat had never done business with a merchant who remained bound by the laws of the Church, and he wasn't sure of etiquette, if there was any. He glanced around, but there were no other customers. He cleared his throat.

The hawker scowled. "Out with it. Or, if you're just going to stand there, tell me now so I can get back to work."

Ranat cleared his throat again. "I'm a friend of Gessa's." His voice was quiet.

"And?"

"She said you might be interested ..." He trailed off and reached into his sack to pull out the belt. Gessa had scraped off most of the mud the night before, and it glittered in the muted light wafting from the door.

The hawker arched bushy eyebrows and, after hesitating a second, picked it up. "This looks like Veshari's work. Where'd you get it?"

"Found it," Ranat said. "And that's the truth, too, so don't look at me like that. I don't know who Veshari is."

The hawker eyed him a moment more, then nodded. "Alright, alright. Veshari was an Artisan –that's Artisan with a capital 'A'—one of the lords of Valez'Mui before he converted to the Church. Now he does custom stuff for the high-ups over in Tyrsh. They love making up their personal emblems over there."

Ranat grunted. "Here, too."

The hawker grinned. "Ain't that the truth? Anyway, don't know who this used to belong to. Definitely someone high ranking."

"So," Ranat said. "How much will you give me for it?"

The merchant looked at the buckle again, frowning in thought. For a while, the only sounds were the murmurs of passersby and the soft dribble of rain drifting in from the open doorway.

"Problem is," the hawker mused with a sideways look at Ranat. "It's more valuable intact. A lot more. Priceless work of art and all that. I could never sell it as is, though. Not something unique like this. That type of thing could come back and haunt me. And damn, would it be heartbreaking to take it apart—like taking a prize camel and turning it into meat." Another sideways look. "I could give you thirty Three-Sides for it, I suppose. For the raw materials."

Ranat reached over and plucked the belt from the man's hands. "The iron alone is worth twice that, at least, and you know it. Gessa didn't tell me you were a schemer."

"Fine, fine. You know what you're doing. Fair enough. Can't blame me for trying. Sixty, then."

"A hundred." Ranat's voice was flat.

"Eighty."

"Ninety."

The hawker chewed his lip, eyeing the belt dangling in Ranat's hand. "Fine," he said again after a minute. "Ninety. Anything else?"

Ranat turned to look out the cluttered doorway, into the rain and the bustling street. "Yeah. Where's an alehouse near here?"

The hawker paused where he'd begun counting out coins. "There's a wine bar a block over," he gestured with his head.

"Anywhere else?"

The hawker shrugged and went back to counting. "I don't know. Probably. People like their wine over here."

Ranat made a face and clutched at his hand; it had begun to tremble. "Never mind. Can't abide wine. I'll walk back to the Lip."

CHAPTER THREE

A WEEK LATER, RANAT'S TIN WAS ALMOST SPENT. He'd given Gessa twenty Three-Sides—twice what he owed her, but he'd felt some undefinable, misplaced guilt, and giving her less hadn't seemed right.

He'd pretty much moved into the nameless bar where he'd met Gessa. What had followed was a blur of long nights, forgotten conversations, and painful mornings, until he'd found himself with enough tin to keep the shakes at bay, but not enough to continue down the spiral he'd started on.

Ale and beer, he thought. *Too expensive.* He should have switched to glogg long before he did. Always the connoisseur.

And now he was being followed.

He hadn't been sure, not at first, but now there was no doubt. He'd started going to different bars, just to check. The same two straight-backed men, looking uncomfortable in their peasants' clothes, their messy hair and carefully layered grime unable to mask the air of confidence they exuded towards the poverty around them. An invisible wall of pride. They didn't look like the Church, but they smelled like it.

Ranat cursed at himself and finished the last swill of glogg. Who knows how long they'd been trailing him. It'd been a week since he'd been sober enough to notice anything.

He glanced down at the silk pouch cradled in his lap. Five, maybe six Three-Sides, a few disks, and a handful of copper balls. Enough to drink for the next few days if he paced himself, but now he had to deal with those two before he could enjoy it.

He pushed his way into the street and headed north. The Lip was maybe a span away, and he could lose them there if they tried to follow him that far. He took a roundabout way, sticking to the most crowded avenues. Boxlike, two-story tenements of limestone leered on either side.

It was the tombs, he repeated to himself. It must be. He'd been getting greedy. A few years ago, he'd found a burial list of some of the founding families. Generations of top Church officials. Old money. He'd hit a few, then try to convince himself to wait a while, but it had been too easy. Easy tin. Easy booze. And every time, he'd think, "This time I'll stretch it out. This time the haul will last a month, maybe two."

But his hauls never lasted that long.

Now, he'd pissed off the wrong family. Someone had found their ancestor's treasures missing and started looking into it. Ranat had always wanted to ask someone: if the highest levels of Heaven were so great that people would pay tens of thousands of Three-Sides in Salvation Taxes every year to get into one, why would they need to be buried with sacks of money? Was there one final tax once you got there?

He glanced over his shoulder, back down the crowded street. If he didn't lose the pair following him, he thought he might get the chance to find out.

Neither were in sight. It was nearing midday, and the clouds were sinking lower, the drizzle thinning to fog. He slowed his pace a little.

Something slammed him from the side, so hard it knocked the wind out of him before he hit the ground. He had no idea where they'd come from. The man that had tackled him got to his feet. Another one stood behind, looking down at Ranat, who lay curled on the wet flagstones, gasping for air.

The first one brushed himself off, muttering curses. "Next time you can be the one that jumps into the goddamn mud," he said to his companion. He was large under the rough, wool peasant garb, with a sand-colored mustache that hid his mouth.

Ranat, through his painful gasps, suspected he was sneering.

The second man, clean-shaven and black-haired, with a forgettable face, said, "Stop complaining. It's not like they're your clothes. If you don't like getting wet, you should've went into a different line of work. Tie him."

He turned to address Ranat as his partner rolled him over and bound his hands. Ranat was faintly aware of a hundred sets of eyes as people gathered around the unfolding spectacle, slowing their pace as they passed, pretending they weren't watching.

"Ranat Trotz," the second man intoned, gaze bored as if reading the words off Ranat's face. "You have been tried, sentenced, and convicted of murder, and struck from the Books of Heaven. Your execution will take place by the will of the Grace of Fom. Until such time, or until dead, you are to be held in the Pit for public viewing. Have you any statements?"

Ranat craned his neck to look up at the faces of the two men staring down on him, and of the mob of onlookers who turned away. The smell of the muddy stone was cool and soothed his lungs, which still burned for air. One word bounced around his head, tightening the knot of panic that was building deep in his stomach—one word that fell out of his mouth before he knew he'd uttered it. *"Murder?"*

CHAPTER FOUR

IMAGES OF RANAT'S FUTURE FLASHED THROUGH his mind as the two men escorted him through the streets. Scenes laced with terror. He knew of the Pit, even if he'd never been the sort that enjoyed that particular brand of entertainment. A drained cistern near the arenas, it imprisoned the worst the Church had to offer, or at least the worst as far as they were concerned. No cells, no guards. Just a hole, open to the sky, where the citizens of Fom could jeer at the condemned two-hundred hands below. The only food in the Pit was whatever onlookers tossed down, rotting and poisoned more often than not, and competition for what few scraps remained was legendary. People called it the Peasant's Arena because the fighting in the Pit could be as good as what the professionals did, and it was free.

Ranat pictured himself at the bottom of that hole, fighting with the others for a few bits of toxic meat or rotting vegetables, of starving to death or dying in the slow, painful convulsions brought about by poison, cast down by a victim's vindictive relative or a bored merchant's son. He imagined surviving long enough to be escorted to the surface again only to be hung in public shame, his name blacked from the Books of Heaven.

Murder. *Murder!* His mind spat the word. All his life, he'd gone by what was right. Maybe not right to everyone, but right to him. He only ever stole what the dead didn't need. He never asked anything from the living. Bargained, but never asked. The thought of murder sickened him, but the thought of being called a murderer filled him with rage. He'd grown up a runaway on the streets of Fom. More than once, it would have made his life easier if he'd killed someone, but he'd always taken the high road. The harder road.

And not out of fear of punishment. Had they convicted him of grave-robbing, the sentence would have been the same, but it would have been a fate he could be at peace with. His own fault. He could come to terms with the consequences of his life's actions—he'd long ago accepted that his life might end that way. It would be an honest execution, at least.

This, though, for his name to be condemned forever for an action that wasn't his, was too much to bear.

He said nothing to his captors. He knew there'd be no point. They were either faithful to Heaven or else well-compensated for the work they did for the Church. Or both. They wouldn't listen to him. They had a job, and they would do it.

Ranat hadn't been paying attention to where they were taking him, but he noticed now. The streets were growing wider, packed with people. Kiosks lined both sides of the boulevard and ahead loomed one of the smaller arenas. People milled in front of the red stone edifice like ants teeming in front of their kicked hill, waiting for the gates to open. They were taking him straight to the Pit.

He knew this shouldn't surprise him. They had told him his trial and sentence had taken place without him. Still, he'd envisioned ... *something*. A holding cell. A guardhouse. A torture chamber, even. Anything that would delay the inevitable.

Anything.

Ranat, who until now had allowed the pair to lead him along, leaped backward into the man behind him, who had been guiding the broken old man with only a hand resting on his shoulder.

The guard stumbled, tripped over his own heel, and fell. Ranat tumbled down on top of him. Adrenaline surged, and Ranat twisted to his feet, hands still bound behind him, and ducked his second captor's tackle.

I'm an old man, Ranat thought. *They're young, and I'm old. They can take me any time they want.*

But they didn't. Instead, the second man's missed tackle made him trip over the first guard before he could get to his feet, and again they both ended up on the ground in a tangle of arms and legs.

Ranat ran.

They can catch me, he thought. *I'm an old man. My hands are tied. Everyone will point out whichever way I go, and they'll catch me. If I'm lucky, they'll decide I'm not worth the bother, and they'll kill me in the street.*

He continued to run, weaving through throngs of people, dodging down this street and that alley, falling, scrabbling to his feet, and running again. Shouts and general discord welled behind him, but grew further away, until they faded into the mumbling voice of the city.

Eventually, his burning lungs and rubbery legs forced him to stop. Fighting for breath, he slumped to the ground next to a copper grate, green with verdigris and billowing warm, humid air. He was in an alley. The flagstones—they were flagstones and not cobbles here—were clean and puddled with rainwater. There was no one else around, though somewhere nearby, he could hear carriages and wagons trundle along. He had no idea where he was. The clouds had lifted high again, giving the false promise of sun.

He looked around for a piece of glass or something he could use to cut the bonds from his hands. No glass, but a jagged copper pipe jutted up from the alley floor two hands high, as if it had been cut off not long ago. The edge of it still gleamed in the grey light, untouched by corrosion.

Ranat scooted over and scraped his bonds over the pipe until they loosened and broke, praying the whole time the valve connected to it wouldn't start belching white-hot steam onto his back. He couldn't believe he'd escaped, and the thought of doing so only to be scalded to disfigurement and death in an alley didn't sit well.

Hands free, he slumped against the wall, thinking. His left wrist was bleeding. The cut looked too clean to have happened on the pipe, but he didn't know where else he might have gotten it. Blood dribbled onto the cuff of his white coat and added a new stain. Ignoring the chill draft that wafted onto his chest, he tore a strip from his shirt and bound the slash as best he could with his free hand.

He needed to get out of the city, but he wasn't sure where. Except by sea, Fom was isolated, and he'd never be able to sneak through customs to the docks. Past the vineyards, the coast to the south was empty. The city of Maresg lay to the north, but he wasn't sure how far, and he knew enough to know the roads had been abandoned centuries ago after it had declared itself free from the Church, and no one had bothered to stop it. Dirigibles went that way sometimes, up the coast, but he had no way of boarding one. The mountains that backed Fom to the east had only one pass, and there was nothing but wasteland on the other side.

South would be best. There'd be fishing villages, anyway. From there, he could spend the rest of his tin —which the Church thugs hadn't bothered to take from him—on passage to Maresg. He'd be safe there.

He'd never see Gessa again. That thought brought a bigger pang of regret than he'd expected, but he reminded himself if he left, she'd be safer too.

Ranat wandered with the ebb and flow of the crowd until he figured out where he was. After a few blocks, he got his bearings and felt a slight pang of relief to find he'd already been going south. It was mid-afternoon, maybe later. The buildings along either side had facades of marble, and some of the larger structures sported green copper domes more prevalent around Wise Hall, which lay to the east and south.

To be on the safe side, he left the main avenue again, keeping further west until he came to where warehouses and kiosks of fruit vendors and fishmongers lined the streets. And bars.

He licked his lips and looked up at the narrow belt of sky slashed between buildings as if he could discern the position of the sun. The clouds had come down again, and rain had started falling in earnest. It was darker than it had been, but he'd lost all track of time and didn't know if it was dusk or the clouds had just gotten thicker. At least, he thought, he'd be able to see the sun once in a while after he left Fom.

A brass vent began to whistle steam from the ground behind him.

He told himself there was a risk that it wasn't yet dusk, and he'd have an easier time leaving the city after dark. To be safe, he'd just pop in somewhere for a drink or two. Until it was night.

————

It had been dark for over three hours, but it took four for Ranat to notice. The inn he'd chosen, which had a sign depicting what looked like a duck sitting on a bed, but for some reason, customers called The Leaky Barrel, had a guestbook resting on one corner of the bar. No one seemed to have any interest in signing it, nor had they, it appeared, in years. Ranat spent the time sipping a heinous concoction of glogg while he paged through it. Names and dates spanned twenty years and more. Ranat wondered who they were, where they'd come from, why in the Heavens they'd ended up in The Leaky Barrel, or had the urge to sign the worn leather guestbook. Or, for that matter, why they didn't anymore. He'd thought about trying to take it with him, but it was too big to carry around, and it could never join his collection anyway, which now lay abandoned.

The thought made him sad, prompting him to turn away from the guestbook and look out the window. Night covered Fom.

He swilled what was left in his cup and rose, wobbly, to his feet. The bar had grown busier while he'd sat there lost in the list of names, and a mix of warehouse workers and well-dressed professionals ignored him as he staggered out the door.

It was late enough that the streets in this part of town were empty. The rain had lifted, but fog had rolled in. The intermittent glow lamps created isolated pools of pallid radiance. Ranat stumbled, first from one side of the street, then to the other, as he traversed from one island of light to the next.

The events of that day were hazy—like a dream he'd been convinced was real, but was now a fractured, confused memory. More than once, he checked his wrist, half expecting there to be no cut or, if there was, to remember where he'd gotten it. But every time it was there, and only one harsh memory stood out.

Murder.

The street became first a gentle slope, then a hill, then a mountain. Fog turned back to rain, then to fog again as he climbed towards the ridge that drew the edge of the city. The road grew wider, the buildings spread out until they evolved into separate estates, complete with gatehouses and wooded gardens.

He continued. Above the fog, the hill still rose another two-hundred paces before ending at a black ridgeline, above which a few stars twinkled. His legs ached, his heart pounded, and cold sweat trickled down his back. He couldn't stop, wouldn't look back.

And then, there he was. Below and in front, the hated vineyards. Long, neat rows of vines, green with leaves but still bare of fruit, marched like ranks of drunken soldiers down to the cliffs, broken only by the occasional farmhouse or servant dorm. Beyond, the sea shone—an endless void, even the whitecaps rendered invisible by distance and the blackness of night.

He hadn't been here in years. He used to come, a long time ago, sneaking through the vines every year to see his sisters and brother. He never risked speaking to them or even let them see him, but he'd come. Just to watch. First every year, then every few, until now. He didn't remember the last time he'd come up this ridge, but he'd been younger then. Younger by far.

He hated them back then. Blamed his parents for his life planting vines and picking grapes. Blamed his siblings for the guilt he'd felt after he left.

Ranat looked down at the dark shapes of the farmhouses, silhouettes in the gloom, but he could still see them as a nine-year-old boy, cursing their existence. Red-tile roofs and rough stone walls. Lacquered shutters painted green or orange. He was a stupid child back then, blind to all but himself, ignorant.

And now he was a stupid old man.

Behind him, Fom, the biggest city in the world, lay blanketed by its eternal fog, all its splendor reduced to a fuzzy mass of yellow. A bed of spoors coughed from the lungs of some luminous troglodyte.

He flopped down onto a flat boulder squatting at the side of the road and looked over the city. The mass of fog wasn't quite featureless. There, in the distance, just at the edge of his sight, the Customs Towers that lined the harbor poked up through the mist, their bronze tops glittering in the diffused amber light spread below them.

The ghosts of his past haunted him. On one side, the vineyards. Parents he'd abandoned to slavery. Siblings, now as dead as his mother and father, who'd stayed on despite their suffering, lest they lose the petty Heaven of Stone they'd earned after a lifetime of misery.

On the other side, Fom. The life he'd chosen, Heaven and his family be damned. He realized that what he'd always feared most was an obscure death—passing on in solitude, a nameless body for a beggar to loot in some trash-strewn alley.

Now, they'd taken even that. Obscurity was lonely, but it was better than infamy. A few weeks ago, no one knew who Ranat Totz was. Now his name was stricken from the Books of Heaven. Ranat Totz was a murderer. And not a murderer with a misguided, noble cause, but a petty thug who'd stabbed a man in the heart for his money.

Ranat felt anger again well like bile. He'd always believed an honest life, at least honest to himself, was worth living. Now, he thought, what do all those years of honesty mean, if for an eternity afterward, he would only be remembered for a crime that wasn't his?

He looked again down at the vineyards, willing himself to continue his exile, but it was a hollow thing now, his will. What's within a name? Nothing and everything. Nothing, because as long as you're alive, a name is just what people call you. Everything, because after you're gone, it's all that's left.

The name Ranat Totz was tainted now, all so some smuggler or black-market thug could live his life in peace after a deal gone bad.

He scrubbed at the tears that soaked his face and dripped from his gnarled beard. His whole life, he now saw, had been pointless, selfish. A quest for easy money. One drink after another. Every moment of his life had existed only for the next. Fearing obscurity while doing nothing to avoid it, until just his name remained. And now, that was gone, too.

Well, he thought. Fuck that. His whole life had

been an easy way out, and now there was nothing left. But it wasn't too late.

He wiped his eyes again, scoured his face with his hands, took a deep breath. The night air smelled of rain and salt water.

Ranat Totz began walking towards Fom.

CHAPTER FIVE

THE HAWKER FELL TO HIS KNEES, WEEPING.
"Forgive me! Heaven, forgive me," he burbled.
"Please. I didn't have a choice."

Ranat looked around, uncomfortable. It was mid-morning; he hadn't slept in two days and was beginning to regret his decision to come to the hawker first. He was glad there were no other customers around to see this display, but he worried about what might happen if one came in.

"Look," he said. "I'm not—"

"They made me tell them who I got the belt from. They said—"

"Wait. Just hold on. I—"

"—raising my Salvation Taxes again, and—"

"Stop, listen to—"

"—going to kill me—"

"*Shut up!*" Ranat whipped out his left hand, which connected with the hawker's round face. The hawker fell back with a shriek, clutching his nose but, to his credit, stopped talking. Ranat looked down at his left wrist, which had started bleeding again with the impact. He swore to himself and looked around for something to wrap it in. He was shaking. Need a drink, he thought. Just one, so he could think.

The hawker cowered, lowering his face and whimpering.

"I'm not going to hurt you," Ranat said as calm as he could. "Er, again."

"What do you want?" The hawker's voice was nasal and muffled around the hand, still holding his nose. Indignant irritation had replaced the fear in his voice.

"Tell me what happened. Slowly."

The hawker took a deep breath. "Two Church men showed up here the day after you came in. I hadn't even had a chance to take apart the damn belt. They found it, asked where I'd got it from. I told them the truth: you were a guy I'd never done business with before and didn't know who you were. But they pressed."

Ranat froze. "What did you tell them?"

"That you were a friend of Gessa's."

"You got Gessa involved?" Ranat's voice was icy.

"No, no, no. Well, yeah, but she's fine." The hawker drew in a shuddering breath and swallowed when he saw Ranat's face grow darker. "I swear. She's fine. She just helped me with something yesterday. They just watched her until they found you. I thought they ... how did you ...?" He swallowed again.

"If you're lying ..."

"Fine, fine. I'm not lying."

"So, what about the belt?" Ranat demanded. "Who did it belong to?"

"What do you mean? I didn't *not* tell you anything. Someone high up. Beyond that, how the hell should I know? There's three-thousand personal seals floating around the Church. You think I can name three of them?"

Ranat sighed and leaned back, grasping his shaking hands. "Yeah. Okay. Alright. You're right. Sorry. Sorry about your nose." He sighed again. "Sorry."

Then he turned away and disappeared into the crowded street.

———

It was late afternoon before Ranat found Gessa, idling in front of the alehouse. He watched her from the mouth of an alley not much wider than his shoulders, a little way further down the road, and ducked his head back into the shadows every time she looked in his direction.

He wanted to talk to her—hadn't known how much he'd wanted to talk to her until he saw her standing there, but he knew they must still be watching her. She was how they had found him the first time. They were looking for him now, and she was the only connection they had. Her, and he'd realized too late, the hawker.

Apparently, they hadn't considered Ranat going straight to the man that had ratted him out. He'd gotten lucky on that one, and he knew it. He wasn't about to blow it now. Not until he did what he had to do.

It looked like Gessa was waiting for someone, but the longer he watched her, the more he wondered. Was she waiting for him? He felt the hairs stand up on the back of his neck at the thought. If they were watching her, and she was waiting for him ... however he looked at it, it didn't look good. He hoped she wasn't in on it, too. Even if she hadn't had a choice, the thought was more than he could take.

He decided he'd rather not know, and he slipped away again, while Gessa continued to wait through the deepening shadows, the glow lamps flaring on around her.

———

The Library of Heaven, known more often as just The Library, was a wide, squat tower of volcanic glass, cyclopean and out of place next to the delicate white-and-rose buttresses of Wise Hall and the adjacent palace.

The Library held the names of every person in Fom who had ever belonged to the Church of N'-narad, and which level of Heaven they would attain, or which they were in now. A permanent tax record.

Ranat had mixed feelings about The Library. Despite his fascination with reading lists of names, he'd never been there before, although it was open to the public once a week. There were no Salvation Taxes for a grave robber, and even if there had been, he didn't think he would have paid them.

Still, he'd been raised with the Church, and he'd always carried an inkling of a feeling that his casual disdain of the N'naradin tax system had doomed him to the Void. Or worse, now that he'd been stricken from the Books, condemned to endless suffering.

He'd swallowed his thirst and spent most of his last tin on a new linen shirt, this one dark grey, and rough wool pants. He also got a new coat. As much as he'd grown to love the other one, he needed to concede that it was a bad idea to wear a blood-stained coat that once belonged to a dead official he'd been convicted of murdering into the heart of Church power. The new clothes felt stiff and strange, and Ranat realized they were the first clothes he'd worn in fifty years that hadn't come from the dead.

He'd shaved, too, back in his basement, after he'd watched the place for a day and decided no one was lurking around, waiting for him to come home. He'd watched people shave with flint razors before. It looked easy enough, but a dozen tiny, random gashes now sliced his face. He'd spent more than a day sleeping, but when he left for The Library the next morning, they still burned raw. His tarnished mirror revealed a ragged-haired old man with tired, sad eyes and scarred jowls. His flesh was grey, except for the dozen small bloody cuts and his ruddy, bulbous nose. Ranat felt even more conspicuous than before.

On the road up to Cathedral Hill and through the gates, he was ignored. Just another old peasant, dressed in the best he had, come to see his name in the Books before he died.

The Library was a vast corkscrew, each chamber within vaulted and walled with leather-bound books. Every room linked to a central spiral stairway. Nineteen vaults in all, from the base to the top. A vault for each Heaven, and one more for people like Ranat, bound for the purgatory of the Void for never paying their Salvation Taxes.

No, he reminded himself. One more for people like he'd *used* to be. Now his name wasn't in any book at all.

Ranat paused at the base of the stairs. The towering entrance lay behind him, an arch of basalt carved into knots of thick rope, held aloft by square pillars and polished until the steady stream of visitors could see themselves reflected in the gleaming, black surfaces. Souls drowning in darkness.

Stairs in front of him, white marble, circled the wall all the way to the Sun-and-Moon mosaic glinting in the ceiling, made of countless chips of glass and bronze. Walls were likewise marble, set with hundreds of gloomy bas-reliefs of people Ranat didn't recognize. The broad double doors that followed the stairs up, all propped open, were cut from gleaming blocks of volcanic glass.

Soldiers in white and red dress uniforms patrolled the stairs and the various landings, sometimes answering questions from the parishioners, but mostly looking bored. Ranat kept his head down as he clambered up the steps, but none of them paid him any more heed than they did any of the other peasants.

The vast majority of visitors from the city disappeared into one of the first two vaults, representing the lowest levels of Heaven, on opposite sides of the ground floor. He didn't go into either of them, but he could see through the doorways, which rested ajar on enormous stone hinges. The lower vaults were huge —half the size of the rest of The Library, lined with tomes containing tiny names and birth dates. He wondered how one person could find a name penned in one of those tomes. Just one in a list of millions.

Ranat still didn't know who he was looking for. He did, however, know that the man he hadn't murdered was a high-ranking Church official, recently deceased, whose personal seal was a phoenix. He decided he'd start looking at the top.

The higher levels were almost vacant compared to the swarming mass going in and out of the lower two vaults. One guard, dressed in all white, with the Sun-and-Moon of the Church embroidered in red over his heart and larger on his back, leaned on the marble railing, looking down on the crowds below, distant thoughts etched on his face.

As Ranat ascended the stairs, the man stood straight and watched as the old man approached. "The lowest vaults contain the lowest books of Heaven," the guard explained as if he couldn't imagine why Ranat would progress any further into The Library.

Ranat's mind turned to how bad he needed a drink. A flask of rum rode in his pocket, almost half full, but he knew now would be a bad time to take a swill from it. He cleared his throat and tried to adjust his posture so he'd look like he knew what he was doing.

"Found my name," he mumbled. "And a few others I'd been meaning to see. Just thinking, since I was here, I'd see who got themselves into the Highest

Books over the years. I mean, besides the Grace and the Bishop. Who else gets to be up there?" He nodded toward the stairs leading up past the guard. "That is," he added, "if us common folk are allowed."

The guard eyed him with tired disdain, a local giving directions to a tourist. "Yeah, fine. Go ahead." He went back to leaning on the railing, watching the crowd, old man already forgotten.

Ranat nodded his thanks to the man's back and proceeded up the stairs. None of the other guards bothered with more than a glance at the grandpa who stumbled up the steps past them, gasping for breath and limping on tired legs.

The top-most vault, housing the names of those bound for the Heaven of Light, was still massive, although perhaps a twentieth the size of one of the lower ones. Yellow stained glass banded around the top of the room, turning the dull grey light of Fom into a facsimile of sunshine. The books in here were thinner, but broader and square, about three hand-lengths to a side. A few visitors lurked around, paging through old tomes or walking between the shelves, running fingers across the leather spines, their reverence shouted through their silence. To one side sat two ornate oak tables ridged with vines and flowers. On each lay an immense book, eight hands to a side, almost as thick. Above one, a sign read: "Book of Bishops." Above the other: "Book of Graces."

Ranat wondered if that meant the Graces and

Bishops got into an even higher level of Heaven. The thought made him snort a humorless laugh.

An ancient scribe in red-and-black robes with thick white hair glanced up from the desk by the door as Ranat entered, but turned back to his work without a word. The man had a scrawled list in front of him and was penning the names from it into a new tome. Ranat saw, with a fresh glimmer of hope, that after he penned each name, he selected a signet from an array set in glass cases around the desk. These he dipped in ink before stamping them next to the entries. Every seal in the Church linked to every name.

Ranat looked around the room, hesitated, and turned back to the scribe. He fiddled, and when the old man didn't look up again, he cleared his throat. The rough sound echoed off the vaulted ceiling, and he winced at the sound.

"Yes?" The whisper was harsh and almost as loud as Ranat's cough. A few people glared in their direction.

"I'm, uh, looking for, um, someone. They, uh ..." He trailed off under the scribe's withering glower.

"Yes?" The man hissed again, even louder than before. "Out with it!"

"Someone within the Church died not long ago, and I want to pay my respects," Ranat blurted the words as fast as he could in a graveled hiss. In his coat pockets, he clenched his fists to keep his hands from shaking.

The scribe nodded toward the wall opposite the Books of Graces and Bishops. There was another table with another book on it, this one's size more in keeping with the others. Above it, a sign read: "Book of Life."

Ranat looked at it, then at the man, who had already turned his attention back to his work. "Um. If he's recently passed on ...?" He trailed off again.

The scribe looked up, rolled his eyes, and nodded a second time towards the book.

"Uh," Ranat whispered. "Thank you."

Ranat went over to the Book of Life and opened it, half-expecting a shout of alarm as he touched the tomb, but the room remained quiet below the susurration of turning pages.

The Book of Life was different than the others in the room, despite its identical size; beyond a simple list of names and seals, brief obituaries were printed beneath each name.

Ranat swallowed, waiting to be grabbed by a guard lurking invisible behind him. The room remained calm.

He panned down the names, working backward. With the short obituaries, there were only ten names to a page. Ranat wondered how long someone had to be dead before they were transferred to a normal book, and what they would do with this Book of Life when a new one was full.

He found the phoenix on the third page back.

Angular and stylized, there was no mistake. He hugged himself as he read, shaking hands balled into fists and tucked into his armpits.

Hierophant Trier N'navum, Born Nir 7699 - Died Ageus'tan 7747.

Third Hierophant under Arch Bishop Daliius III. His position was often seen as the most difficult of the Five; it fell on him to restructure troubled posts in the most distant reaches of the N'naradin Fold. He is survived by his brother Lem; his soul rests in the Heaven of Flowers.

Ranat stepped away from the book, his quivering hands itching to reach for the flask of rum tucked in his pocket. He forced himself to drop his arms to his side and walk from the vault, then down the long stairs and out of The Library, pace unhurried, expression calm.

He forbade himself the flask until he was out of the compound at the top of Cathedral Hill and tucked away into one of the narrow, steam-filled streets of Grace's Parish. There, he took a long pull and frowned. He thought there was more in it than that.

He'd been worried about being accused of killing some random official, but the man had been a damn Hierophant. Calling him "high-up" didn't cover it.

When he'd taught himself to read as a child, sneaking books out of the Vintner's office, he'd often done so with books about the Church. They weren't stories of the Heavens—the Vintner was nothing if not a secular man—but charts and lists of the hierarchy. Ranat probably knew more about the Church's structure than any other peasant, and most of the merchants, too. The problem was, now that he knew who he was accused of killing, he had more questions and no answers.

The Hierophants operated under the Arch Bishop's direct command to bring local governments in line. Trier N'navum couldn't have been here for that. Fom was no distant provincial outpost. It was, well, Fom—three times larger than the capital city of Tyrsh, and the Grace of Fom was the second in command of the Church.

Trier N'navum could have been in Fom for any number of reasons. Meeting with the Grace or just passing through the port on the way to some far-flung prefecture along the coast. None of that, though, explained what one of the most powerful members of the Church was doing in an alley by the Lip, all by himself, in the middle of the night.

Ranat drained the flask, then shook it next to his

ear, hoping there might be one swallow left that didn't flow into his mouth with the rest of it.

Then he sighed, stuffed the empty bottle into his pocket, and began trudging home, questions swimming through his mind.

CHAPTER SIX

RANAT CROUCHED IN THE ALLEY WHERE HE'D found the body of Hierophant Trier N'navum, staring at the muddy cobbles, trying to force answers from them through strength of will.

There was, of course, no sign that a body had ever lain here. It was a little after noon. The clouds were high and bright, granting a rare reprieve from the drizzle. Deep within the shadows of the narrow street, a vent to the Tidal Works gasped. Behind him trundled wagons and pedestrians, and the chorus of beggars who'd emerged from the nearby tunnels of the Lip.

He sighed, and the sound bubbled in his chest. That couldn't be good, he thought. He'd slept a little in an abandoned squat a few blocks from his room after he'd left the Library, afraid to go home in case the Church was watching. But his mind had been too aswarm with questions that had no answers to get much rest. He felt like he'd aged twenty years in the week since he'd first found the body. For an old man, that was saying a lot.

Ranat didn't know what he was looking for. He just knew there needed to be some clue to what the Hierophant had been doing, who he'd been meeting. Who had killed him. There had to be, or else it wasn't fair.

No footprints, no dropped confessions, no hidden murder weapons. Nothing that would tell the world Ranat Totz was an innocent man. As he conceded it, he fought back the welling tears. Not fair. None of it.

Out in the street, life continued. "Tin? Spare any tin? Just a ball or a disk? Excuse me, sir. Excuse me, miss." The song of the beggars droned on. Ranat wondered if they ever stopped. Wondered if they ever left this dismal strip of the Grace's Walk, where, inexplicably, they'd decided to converge in some distant past, and had come here every day ever since.

He wiped his face with a filthy hand, leaving a smear of mud unnoticed on his stubbled cheek, and took a pull from a fresh rum bottle. A full one, not just a flask. It had left him with one last Three-Side and a few balls, but at least it would last him more than a day. Hopefully.

Most of the beggars were children. He knew their keepers waited for them back in the tunnels, that of the tin they to made every day, they kept none of it. The merchants knew it too, which is why the nicer ones gave them a pull off the glogg keg along with a couple copper balls. A little something for themselves.

Still, the system worked well enough for their handlers to send them here, to the same stretch of Grace's Walk. Every day. And every night.

Ranat took a few steps into the street and waved the rum bottle at the nearest beggar—a boy of about ten, wearing tattered, muddy pants so filthy it was impossible to tell what sort of material they were. He had no shirt or shoes at all.

"Were you here before dawn, a week or so ago?" Ranat asked, shaking the rum bottle again for good measure.

The kid said nothing but nodded toward the bottle. Ranat handed it to him.

The boy took a long pull from it, wincing as it burned down his throat, and handed it back to Ranat, wiping a dirty forearm across his mouth. "No," he said and gave a mean-spirited laugh before darting back into the street around a rumbling keg wagon, dodging a camel that tried to bite him.

Son of a bitch, Ranat thought. He didn't bother going after him. Even if he'd had the energy, he would have let it go. It was too much like something he would have done. Kids living on the street got their dues where they could.

He felt the weight of the bottle, sighed. The boy must have had a big mouth for a little kid. Well, he thought, lesson learned.

He raised the bottle again, and a girl who'd watched the first transaction came over. She was older than the boy. Somewhere in the awkward, gangly years between adolescent and adult. Her body under the rough burlap tunic was skinny, the first hints of womanhood touching her hips and breasts, but her face was unlined and young. Her eyes, though, were hard, ancient.

He asked her the same question. She, like the boy before her, said nothing and nodded toward the bottle. The mannerism was so similar, Ranat wondered if they were siblings. "No, no. Nice try. Tell me first, then we'll see."

She looked like she might protest, but just stuck out her lower lip in a pout. "Fine. No, I wasn't here. Give me a drink or a few tin, and I'll tell you who was, though."

"Tell me, first. Then I'll give you something."

"And how do I know you won't just screw me after you get what you want?"

Ranat scowled. "I guess you don't."

The girl glared at him, jutting her lip out even further, but she didn't leave.

"Look at me," he said. "Do I look like a merchant out to fuck you over? I'm no better off than you, and I never have been. Either tell me or don't, so I can get on with it and ask someone else."

She looked at the bottle again, and Ranat felt an unexpected tug of guilt. She looked at a bottle of rum the same way he had when he was her age. The girl had nothing but a hard life ahead of her, and he was helping her into the ditch.

"Fine," she said before he could think about it anymore. "I got a friend. He's not here now, but he's been doing the nights for the past month. Older than me. Maybe eighteen, twenty. Mass of hair and a beard like polished copper, even when it's wet, which it is all the time out here. Give me a swig off that bottle, and I'll tell you where to find him."

Ranat looked down at the girl, who glared up at him, looking like she was ready to punch him in the neck as soon as he refused her request.

"You know, girl," he said, showing off his missing teeth with a hawkish smile. "You keep that attitude up, and your life will be a lot easier than mine was." He handed her the bottle.

————

The copper-haired man that the girl had called Lint spent his days sleeping somewhere in the maze of the Lip. Ranat had wondered aloud about waiting until the night when he might come out for his shift, but the girl had advised against it. The Grace's Walk was just one of the streets where the keepers sent their vagabonds to congregate, and she didn't know when Lint would be back at the same spot.

Ranat had no reason not to believe her. She'd become friendly enough after he'd handed her the bottle, and he forced himself not to snatch it out of her hand when she'd lifted it for a second, long drink. She explained to him as best she could where Lint slept, and Ranat had left it at that.

The tunnels of the Lip were crowded and twisted, and they stank. Smoke and brine, sweat and sex, death and shit and piss and rotten fish; all of it came together in the passages to turn the air into an overbearing ichor; poison gas that failed to kill, but made Ranat sick every time he went below.

Which is why, even after over fifty years living around the Lip, he'd only been inside a handful of times. A mix of natural tunnels and caverns, and ancient quarries mined out when the city above had been constructed millennia ago; passages not filled with Tidal Works' machinery had become a habitat for the desperate and depraved. Ranat thought if he were to give up now and went into hiding deep within the Lip, the Church would never find him. The authorities never ventured far into the tunnels.

Entrances pocked the muddy streets above, sometimes nothing more than a shoulder-wide hole with a rickety wooden ladder or a stairway that looked to go into a basement, but then kept going. The girl's instructions led Ranat to one such stairway, not far from the high cliffs that marked Fom's precarious northwestern border. He could hear the incoming tide crashing against the limestone as he descended the stairs but, as soon as he was within, the sound became a loud indistinct rush of noise, directionless and all-encompassing.

The press was absolute, and Ranat was at the mercy of its currents. The girl had made it sound easy enough, but travel against the flow of people seemed impossible in the narrow space. It carried him opposite the way he wanted to go until the swarm of humanity deposited him in a large rectangular room with a ceiling so low, he needed to stoop. Dozens of rickety kiosks, selling everything from clothes sewn from rags to pickled fish, formed crooked rows. The air was stagnant, pungent with smoke that sputtered from torches and tar-fuel lamps lining the walls.

Ranat had little choice but to wait near the passage that had ejected him. He would never find his way if he tried to take an alternate route. A nearby kiosk sold glogg, and he paid the woman behind it the last of his tin balls to fill his empty rum bottle. He scowled at the first swallow, almost spit it out, but he didn't. Glogg could be made from pretty much anything, but this was the first time it had tasted like fish.

After a period of time that Ranat measured in swallows of fishy glogg, the tide of humanity sputtering from the passage ebbed, then halted, and began to flood the other way. He gripped his bottle and pressed in with the others.

After that, it was as easy as the girl said it would be. The nest of beggars was in a natural cavern only fifty paces from the stairway where he'd entered. It had taken him long enough that most of the people had woke by the time he got there, getting ready for their shifts, dressing or drinking jars of cloudy water, or eating unidentifiable meat off flat, thin slabs of shale that served well enough as plates.

The man named Lint was just sitting up on his bed mat, rubbing his eyes and looking around groggily at the others. He was the first to see Ranat, who stood in the chamber's mouth, staring at him. He arched his eyebrows when he noticed the attention, but didn't seem concerned by it.

Ranat wavered a moment and shambled into the room, stumbling and almost falling on top of a young girl who squealed in alarm. The fish-glogg was stronger than he'd given it credit for.

The others in the room looked on with passing interest as Ranat picked his way over to Lint, careful not to trip over anyone else.

Lint watched him approach, scratching his beard. "Yeah?"

Ranat sat next to him without invitation and handed him the bottle.

Lint took it, uncorked it, and took a whiff, then frowned at it and handed it back without drinking.

Ranat shrugged, took a pull from it, and jammed the cork back into the neck. It wasn't that bad once you got used to it.

"You were on the Grace's Walk before sunrise a week or two ago?"

Lint shrugged. "Where you hear that?"

Ranat paused. "A girl working up there now. She never told me her name. Told me to find Lint, though. I'm guessing that's you."

Lint glowered under his beard. "Smart girl, not giving her name. Wish she didn't tell you mine, neither. Yeah, okay. So? What about it?"

"Just looking for someone who saw something is all."

Lint snorted. "Yeah? Well, you'll have to be more specific."

"A rich guy. Church. White coat, black hair. Meeting with someone in an alley just off where you guys go. Probably a little before dawn. A couple hours, anyway. Not before."

Lint thought. "You got tin?"

Ranat hesitated. He had a lone Three-Side left, hidden in the silk pouch under his coat. "I got fish-glogg."

Lint let out a laugh, despite himself. Then he sighed. "Alright, old man. You win. Give me that bottle."

Ranat offered him the bottle again. Lint took a long swallow, squinched his face as if he were trying to keep from throwing up, and passed it back. Ranat took another swallow himself for good measure.

"No. Nothing like that rings a bell. You sure about when it happened? For the past week, I been further up near the north gate. Few weeks before, I was on the Walk, but the matron had me way down near the Customs Towers."

Ranat frowned, rubbed his jaw, and absently took another drink. When *had* he found the Hierophant's body? The time between then and now oozed in his mind—a hazy string of sleepless nights and empty bottles. Had it been more than a week or two? Had it been a month? Maybe those times he'd slept, he'd slept longer than he'd thought. A day here. Two days there. It added up, and it had happened before. More often than he could count. He'd never had much use for keeping track of time.

He felt Lint's eyes on him, tired, curious, but not malicious. The beggar had never witnessed a meeting like the one Ranat was describing. Maybe Lint had been there, and just not noticed two or three men standing in the darkness of the alley.

Frustration, long building, erupted inside Ranat. The cavern swam in his vision, became a blurry con-stellation of torchlight and faces as tears came unchecked. No one had seen anything. The beggars would have been focused on their quarry in the street, not a secret meeting in the alley. He resented himself for believing there'd been a chance. Even if one of them had seen something, they would have looked away, pushed it from their mind. People living on the streets of Fom didn't live long when they noticed meetings like that. That should have occurred to Ranat, of all people.

"I th-thought ... I-I ... Sorry ..." Ranat stammered and stood, too fast. The room beyond his tears spun and threatened to throw him back on the ground, but he staggered back and forth a few times across Lint's bed and regained his footing. He swayed where he stood, making little circles in the air with his body while his legs stayed put, but at least the danger of falling had passed.

"You okay there, old man?" Lint's concern sounded genuine.

Ranat didn't trust himself to speak, so he only gave a slight nod. The gesture sent the cavern spinning again, but not as bad as standing up had. He took a fumbling step toward the mouth of the chamber. Fresh air, he thought. I just need fresh air, and maybe a drink that doesn't taste like fish.

"Well, hmm ..." Lint said behind him.

Something in his tone made Ranat stop and half turn back.

"I mean, I didn't see a meeting or anything, like the one you said, but ..."

"Yeah?" Ranat's voice came out a hoarse whisper, and he didn't trust himself to look at Lint. He was shaking again, this time with shame. Until a few weeks ago, he hadn't cried in sixty years. He felt the pity in the eyes of those watching him. Felt it make his face grow red.

"Well, just that, now that you made me think on it, there was this keg wagon. A real banged up one, painted green, came rolling along like it was off to put out a fire. Damn camel pulling the thing tried to bite me when I didn't jump out of the way fast enough.

"Anyway, like I said, there was no meeting, but they pulled the wagon up to an alley there, right along the Walk, kind of pulled something out of it, and went off again, back the way they came. I remember thinking it was weird to see a keg wagon that time of night with no kegs on it."

Ranat had stopped shaking, forgetting his shame. He looked at Lint with eyes clearer than they'd been in a long time. "You didn't see what they pulled off?"

"Off the wagon? Nah. I didn't try to, neither. Looked like something that was none of my business. That was all I needed to know."

Ranat pressed his palms into his eyes, let out a deep, shuddering breath. "Looks like you and that girl are both smarter than me, then."

"Huh?"

"Never mind. Did you get a look at the driver?"

"Well, like I say, I tried not to pay attention. Two of them, though. Driver and another one. Hoods up. Heads down. 'Was raining, so nothing weird about that. Both of them big, stocky like. Then again, it was a keg wagon, so nothing weird about that, neither. Anyway, hope it helps."

Ranat took a deep breath and released it. "Yeah. Thanks. It does. Thanks." He turned, paused, and turned back again, digging under his coat for his last Three-Side. "Um, here. I ... thanks."

Lint took it, smiled. "Wow, thank you." He stuffed the coin into his pocket. "And good luck. With ... whatever it is."

Ranat chuckled, his eyes sad. "Whatever it is, it's probably the last goddamn thing I'll ever do. But thanks."

———

The deep grey of evening had been fading when he emerged from the passages, and it was gone before he passed from the Lip into the rest of Fom. Rain dribbled through the night.

Ranat left the Lip and walked. He didn't stop for a drink; didn't stop to think. He walked with only a fraction of his mind knowing where he was going. But he knew enough to stop when he got there.

The thirteen Customs Towers stood over a thousand hands high, topped with bronze domes that sometimes caught sunlight when Fom's fog roiled just right, and the reflections of them shined below: suns burning through the mist. Grass covered the flat ground around them.

He'd heard of other parks in Fom, though he'd never been to any of them, and didn't know where they were. As far as he knew, this was the only place where he could lie in the grass.

If the Eye was out that night, it was too shrouded in clouds to cast its polarized light onto the domes. Light came from the glow lamps that lined the wide boulevards leading from the arches of the Towers into the city. The indistinct grumble of Fom rose behind him over the patter of the rain, while in front of him the ships in the harbor huffed and groaned on the outgoing tide, hidden from view by the limestone cliffs upon which the towers stood.

The muddy grass was cold and slick under his back. Drizzle tickled his face, while an occasional raindrop slapped it. He smelled the rain and the grass, the seaweed of the bay and the ocean beyond, the smoke from the steamships. He was doomed, and he wanted to feel something green and growing one more time.

He was a foolish old man for not seeing it sooner. No, he thought. Not foolish. Just drunk. The Hierophant hadn't gone to the Lip. Someone had dumped him there. They could've taken his tin, his goddamn belt. But they didn't. They left it on his corpse so they could pin whoever looted it with his murder.

They didn't kill him for his money, so why? Ranat could only think of one answer. He was a Hierophant, and someone was tired of his "help."

Ranat was condemned. There was no fighting the Church. He had no proof, and he was a nobody. Lower than a nobody. He was a damn grave robber. He hadn't even been in the Books of Heaven before he'd been stricken from them. There was nothing—

His train of thought skidded to a halt. There *was* something else. Trier N'navum had died with a note hidden in a pocket that his killers must not have known about. Ranat had forgotten about it with everything that had happened. And the endless flood of booze down his throat hadn't helped, either.

He scrambled to his feet and turned his face up into the rain, and let it rinse the mud from his back and hands. Then he pulled himself straight and walked back into the city.

CHAPTER SEVEN

"Never heard of the Crow's Marquis." Gessa paused, eyeing him, curious. "You sure you're okay?"

Ranat had snuck back to his basement and fished out the note he'd gotten off the Hierophant. Then he'd risked ducking his head into the nameless bar, where he'd literally run into Gessa. Her obvious joy at seeing him again, though, was fading into exhausted frustration.

"Yeah," he answered the question for the third time. "I might even get this all sorted if I can ever find this place. How about you? You're okay?"

She shrugged. "I guess. I was worried. You disappeared, and everyone was talking. Then those two guys came around ..."

"Yeah, you said. They didn't hurt you, though?"

"No. Just asked questions that they acted like they already knew the answers to. Not about you, mostly. Just whether I'd seen you. Most of it was about that hawker I introduced you to. I told them what I knew, which wasn't much. They asked where you lived. I lied and said I didn't know. Then they went away."

"What did you say about me?"

"Nothing. Just that I didn't know where you'd gone to. I *didn't* know. Nobody did. After we heard that some official'd been murdered, we thought the Church had picked you up for it, until they started coming around asking about you."

"Haven't seen them around lately?"

"The guys asking the questions, you mean? No. Not in the past week or more. No one else from the Church, either. They caused a stir when they first started hanging around the neighborhood. I would have heard if someone had seen them again."

"Okay. Well." Ranat slid off his stool. "You got these?" He nodded toward the empty glasses on the table.

"I said I did." She frowned and stood alongside him. "Wait a minute—that's it? You show up, make me buy you a few drinks, then you're off again?"

He stopped and looked at her. It never occurred to him she might really care. "Gessa, look." he began and stopped.

She didn't say anything but took a step closer.

"Gessa," he started again. "I don't know how things are going to end up, but ... it was ... good ... I mean with you. It was really good. I wish ... I mean, if things work out, then I'll find you, or whatever. Until then, everyone is still looking for me ... even here. It ... is probably not good. For you, I mean. So, I've got to go. So ... sorry."

Before he could turn, she caught his hand, leaned up, and kissed him. "I'm sorry too," she said. "But I hope you really can work it out." She tried to give him a smile, but the quivering lip gave it away.

"Yeah," Ranat breathed. "Yeah. Me too."

———

"What do you mean I can't go in?"

The man standing in the doorway of The Crow's Marquis was broad enough to fill the frame. He stroked his long black mustache as he spoke. "As I have said, this establishment is a private club. Members only."

"Fine," Ranat grumbled. "You win. I want to be a member."

The man eyed Ranat up and down and adjusted the deep blue kerchief tied around his neck. "Yes. Well. The Marquis is currently ... full."

Ranat rolled his eyes. "Fine."

The Crow's Marquis in a wide maze of streets that twisted between the arenas and Cathedral Hill.

It was once a private estate, and it lay behind a high wall that concealed a flower garden, wooden benches, and a small reflecting pool. Ranat had resorted to asking anyone and everyone if they'd heard of it and, even then, he'd had no success until he'd gone back to the hawker he'd met through Gessa and asked him.

Very prestigious, the hawker had said. He wasn't a member but often thought about becoming one.

If he ever decided to, Ranat would bet they wouldn't be "full."

He exited down the little garden path and onto the flagstones of the street. The bronze gate clanged shut behind him, although he hadn't seen anyone standing nearby. Maybe the doorman had it attached to a string he could pull.

He gazed down the lane. It was a little past noon, and the road was busy but not crowded. Puddles pooled along the creases between the flagstones, but the clouds had lifted again, and a few blotches of pale blue formed and faded away behind the high, wind-blown clouds.

The block stretched long in either direction. The Crow's Marquis hunkered in the middle of a cluster of similar buildings. From what little he could see over the high walls, they looked like houses, but then, so did The Marquis. He wondered how many of them were clubs or brothels, or wherever else the rich whiled away their time.

He circled around, turning left from The Marquis, then left again at the first cross street, then left a third time, hoping to find some sort of forgotten back entrance. Nothing. The alley held a long row of wagon gates, all locked with crossbars from the other side, and he couldn't be certain which one belonged to the Marquis anyway. The walls between the houses ran anything but straight, so it might be more complicated than counting doors. That was presuming he could even open the gate from the outside. He couldn't climb the wall.

Ranat spat onto the flagstones. Nothing was ever easy.

———

He found the hawker later that evening, pulling the heavy oak doors closed across the front of his shop. The man jumped when he saw Ranat, almost dropping his ring of brass keys.

"Oh. Hello. Nice to see you again," the hawker said, sounding very much like he didn't mean it.

"You don't need to pretend to be happy to see me," Ranat stated, standing back to give the hawker enough space to latch the doors together. "But, I need a favor."

The hawker grunted at the bronze lock, which he seemed to be having trouble with, and wiggled the key until there was a soft click. Then he turned, his expression sour. "Yes. A favor. Right." He smirked as he pushed past Ranat into the street.

"Hey." Ranat grabbed the man's arm. "Remember how you ratted me out? How 'sorry' you were when you thought I'd come to get my revenge? Right. And remember how there was no revenge? I just asked a couple of questions. Now, you owe me."

"You hit me," the hawker whined, his voice weak.

"Yeah, and I'm tempted to do it again. Look, I'm not asking for much. At least, hear me out. I don't want you to do anything you don't want to do already, okay?"

"Like what?" The hawker pulled together what was left of his dignity and looked Ranat in the eye.

"Become a member of The Crow's Marquis."

"What? Why?"

"Because I want you to take me there as your servant. Or carriage driver, or whatever. I want to get in and have a look around. That's all. Then I get one last chance to save my ass, and you get to be a member of a prestigious club."

The hawker snorted. "Yeah, until they kick me out for whatever it is you're going to do."

Ranat shook his head. "It's not like that. I won't do anything to embarrass you. If you get me in there, you won't see me again. If I get caught doing something, you can denounce me in front of everyone and leave me to my fate. Fine, okay? Get me in, and the rest is my problem."

The hawker chewed on that for a while. "And what do I get out of it?"

Ranat shrugged. "You get to be a member of one of the most exclusive private clubs in Fom."

The hawker snorted again. "I could do that, anyway."

"Fair enough. Then I promise you, if you do this for me, you will never see me again. Never. And if you don't, I'll come down here and hang around your shop all day. Everyday. Until you change your mind."

"I could have you arrested and dragged away."

Ranat shrugged again. "You could do that now."

The hawker stood in front of the heavy, slatted doors of his shop, staring at Ranat, who was hoping the hawker wouldn't call his bluff.

Finally, the merchant sighed. "I *never* want to see you after this. This is done, and we're even. You can sell your junk to someone else."

Ranat pursed his lips and nodded. "I don't think that will be a problem."

"Give me some time. There's an application process. I don't even know what it involves. Come back here in a week or ten days. If I don't have it by then, I'll at least be able to tell you when I will. Hopefully."

"Fine, then." Ranat let go of the man's arm. "Thanks for this. Oh, one other thing."

The hawker turned from where he'd started down the street. "What?"

"There's a guy who works there. Doorman or bouncer or something. Big guy with a big black mustache."

"And?"

"Well, I'm pretty sure he'll recognize me if he sees me again. Whenever we go, he probably shouldn't be working."

"How the hell should I know when he's working?"

"I don't know. I just thought it would be better if you knew ahead of time."

The hawker rolled his eyes. "Fine. Anything else?"

"Um, yeah."

"What?" The Hawker's voice was growing shrill.

"Do I get to know your name?"

He paused and thought a second. "No," he replied, then wheeled and strode down the street. Rain started to hiss on the cobbles.

Ranat smiled a little at the man's back. "Yeah," he said too soft for the hawker to hear him. "Fair enough. Okay."

CHAPTER EIGHT

RANAT RETURNED TO THE HAWKER'S PLACE ONCE a week for three weeks until he heard back from the Crow's Marquis. There had been multiple tests and five interviews. In the end, they gave the merchant a provisional membership—a fact that made him even more nervous about Ranat's plan, such as it was.

Though he insisted he had done so only for his own self-interest, he had also found out some things he thought Ranat might find useful.

For one, the large man with the mustache was named Lont and was, in fact, the head of security. He kept regular hours and was only there evenings for emergencies and formal events.

The hawker had also learned that servants and the like weren't allowed past the foyer, but that there were always a few there playing cards, waiting for their masters or, if they knew it would be a long night, drinking in the camel sheds behind the house.

Both possibilities sounded fine with Ranat.

———

The hawker, desperate not to lose his hard-earned place in the Crow's Marquis, insisted Ranat take clothes from his shop that would help the old man look like a servant. There was nothing to be done about his missing teeth, but Ranat promised he'd only be opening his mouth to drink, so the hawker consented a change of clothes might be enough.

The doorman that night greeted them with a veneer of respect that bordered on mocking disdain, but the hawker took it cordially enough and left Ranat to wander the foyer and grounds with a final warning look.

The foyer was a long oval, thirty paces across lengthwise, and ten or fifteen between the front door and the reception desk. Windows ran the front of the room, covered by heavy pink and red drapes. The back wall was painted with a recurring red-and-black pattern of angular, interlocking crows. Low, polished tables sat to the left and right of the reception desk, surrounded by tasseled pillows upholstered in gold cloth and embroidered with the same crow pattern. The left table was empty. To the right, two bored-looking men in servants' suits sat playing cards.

The woman at the reception desk eyed him through her thick lashes without looking up from her ledger. Ranat sauntered over. Across from her on the broad desk was the member sign-in book, turned open to the most recent page.

Ranat noted the hawker's name with a small smile and began to thumb backward.

"Excuse me," the woman said, still looking at him through her lashes.

"Oh, sorry," Ranat mumbled. "Just looking for famous names."

She rolled her eyes at him and turned back to her work.

Ranat braved a few more pages until the woman turned her head to eye him directly. "*Excuse me*," she said, the words this time enunciated and dripping with scorn.

"Sorry. Sorry," Ranat said again, throwing his hands up to his shoulders, palms out. "My mistake."

She gave a little snort of derision with a toss of her head and another pronounced eye-roll before looking down at her leger again.

Ranat gave an apologetic nod to the top of her head and went outside.

A brick path ran between the wall of the house and the rampart that bordered the estate next door. Both were covered with ivy, and flowers and patches of grass grew along the path, illuminated with blue-hooded glow lamps poking through the vines. Ranat hadn't seen so much green since he'd left the vineyards.

The Crow's Marquis was a sprawling monster, four stories of stone and white plaster, added onto over the centuries until all original concept of form was lost. Ranat counted two-hundred-and-twenty-nine paces from the front of the house to the back. Where the house ended, the rampart continued for another two-hundred steps, until it stopped at the high alley wall and a pair of wagon gates, one of which looked like it hadn't been opened in fifty years.

The backyard was well-groomed. A massive oak grew to one side, its lower branches brushing the top of the wall that bordered the next estate. Opposite, slumped against the alley wall, was the camel shed. Long and low, it had been pounded together from what seemed to be random chunks of unpolished wood, and someone had made a halfhearted attempt to make it blend in with the delicate artfulness of the rest of the yard by slapping it with green paint.

He couldn't hear any voices coming from the shed, but he had convinced the hawker to buy him a fresh bottle of rum before coming to the club, citing everyone's best interest, and the merchant was practical enough to relent. Ranat didn't have any problem going to the shed and making it a party of one.

The building was dark but unlocked and, if the camel snorting within it was any indication, not devoid of life. Ranat unstoppered the bottle and took a pull. It was too dark to see, but he groped around inside the front gate until he found an oil lantern and the flint hanging on a hook next to it.

The camel snorted in irritation at the sudden flare of light. A row of stables ran down both sides, but only two stalls were full: the grumpy one, a single-humped shaggy black beast who glared at Ranat over the top of the stable door, and the one next to it, where a smaller, sandy-colored animal slept on its feet, oblivious to its neighbor's mood. A scattering of old, moldering straw was strewn around the packed dirt floor. Between the rows of stables sat a single camel-keg wagon that looked like it had been built in the same manner as the barn, with whatever materials were available. It even had the same shade of green paint coating it, though on the wagon, it had worn down to a faint hint of chartreuse brushing the grey wood.

Ranat moved around to the back, careful to avoid both camels by a wide margin. For all he knew, the sleeping one was even meaner.

He climbed into the cart and leaned against the side. He'd been so desperate to get into The Crow's Marquis that he hadn't thought about what he would do once he got here. His original plan had been to go into the bar where the Hierophant had had his last drink and ask around, and he'd never come up with anything else after he'd learned that wouldn't work. He didn't think the hawker would be too keen on asking questions for him—favors from that man were spent.

Ranat had seen the name Trier N'navum in the guestbook before the receptionist had shooed him away, but that didn't do any good. He had no idea if the Hierophant had come here with his killer or separate, or who'd arrived first.

He'd set the bottle down on the wagon bed between his knees, and when he reached down to pick it up, he saw a dark stain, faded but noticeable, spread in a rough circle from where he was sitting. The edges were blurred as if scrubbed. Whatever it was that had soaked into the grain of the wood was a turgid, brownish red.

Ranat jerked upright. The black camel snorted at him, while the other one shifted in its sleep. He bolted from the shed, remembering at the last moment to blow out the lamp so he didn't burn down the building, camels and wagon included.

He trotted over to the back wall of The Crow's Marquis. The kitchen door was propped open to let out the heat from the cooking stoves. Two women stood in the doorway, sampling the fresh air and passing back and forth a rolled stick of magarisi petals, exhaling the sweet smoke out of their noses.

Ranat slowed to a walk when he saw them and sauntered up. They nodded in greeting.

"No party in the camel shed tonight?" a young woman in the sharp suit of a bartender asked.

Ranat smiled. "Not really. Just me." He held out the bottle to them. The one that had spoken shook her head, but her companion, older and dressed in a stained cook's jacket, shrugged, took a drink, and handed it back with a nod of thanks.

"That old keg wagon see much action anymore?" Ranat probed, tone casual.

"Beats me," the cook said. "I'm in the back. Never even see the bar. Cid? How often you need to send Birk out for a pickup?"

Cid shrugged with a little, rueful laugh. "Three, maybe four times a week, just about. Maybe less. Depends. Shit, a few weeks ago, we almost didn't make the run at all."

"Why's that?" Ranat feigned idle interest.

"Some Church official. Came in one evening, requisitioned the wagon. 'Temporary' he said. Thing ended up disappearing pretty well near all night."

"You pick up your kegs at night?"

"Hah! What, you new in town? You want to drive a wagon through Fom during the day, be my goddamn guest."

"Ah, yeah. I guess," Ranat said. "But I've seen plenty of wagons during the day."

Cid scoffed as if the idea were absurd. "Yeah, and they were going nowhere fast, too, I bet."

"Yeah," Ranat agreed. "Fair enough." He paused and offered a quick smile. "So the Church can just come in and take your wagon? Never heard of that before."

Cid took the last drag off the magarisi stick and ground the smoldering roach into the mud next to the door. "If they have the right paperwork, they can. Never heard of it, either, but in he comes—all the right people sign in all the right places, and they can do just about anything they want, I guess. I told him we needed it for a pick-up. He just went straight to the boss, waved the paper at him. Ten minutes later, my keg wagon is rolling out the back gate."

"So, what'd they need the wagon for?" Ranat asked, nonchalant.

Cid shrugged. "Don't know. Wasn't on the form."

Ranat shook his head in disbelief. "Never heard of that before," he said again. "You still got it?"

"What? The requisition form?"

"Yeah."

"Somewhere, yeah." She gave Ranat an incredulous look. "Why? You want to see it?"

"Sure, if it's no trouble."

"Why?"

It was his turn to shrug. "I don't know. I just find shit like that interesting. Not just that the Church can do stuff like that—hell, I know they can do whatever they want—but the fact that they would have to. Seems like they should have their own fucking keg wagons if you know what I mean."

She nodded. "Yeah, it was pretty weird. Sure. Let me see if I can find it. Wait here."

The younger woman, who'd been listening to the conversation in silence, stretched. "I'll go in with you, Cid. I have to get back to work." She gave a little wave to Ranat. "Nice meeting you."

They both disappeared into the back of The Crow's Marquis, leaving the door propped open.

Ranat waited in the darkness of the backyard, heart pounding.

CHAPTER NINE

RANAT HEAVED THROUGH THE BOOKS AND PAPERS stacked around his home, looking for pieces of the black wax seal.

Stupid to have been so careless, he thought. He'd read the note so many times he'd memorized the last message written to Trier N'navum, but until now he'd ignored the clinging fragments of the seal that had held it closed, and every time he'd read it, a few more pieces of it crumbled to his chaotic floor.

There, that was ... no, just another fragment of charcoal. He didn't know where all the charcoal had come from—never even noticed it before until now when he was trying to find something small and black. He'd never considered how filthy his home was; never cared enough to notice.

There. Ranat found the biggest of the wax fragments that had fallen loose, buried under a batch of
faded lumber shipment invoices. He cleared a spot
on the floor, crouched down, and pieced the jigsaw
puzzle together. Not quite half of the original blob
remained, but it hadn't all been there to begin with.
He spent another couple of minutes rifling around
but accepted that he wouldn't find any more among
the filth and clutter. Most of the tree molded onto the
seal was intact, along with a solitary antler branching
up from the remains of some animal's head. Most of
the crescent moon that had been hanging over the
scene was gone. Just a thin splinter of its bottom edge.
He hoped it would be enough.

He folded up the top page of the yellowed
lumber invoice and gathered the wax slivers into it.
Then he folded it again, forming an envelope, and
stuffed it all into his empty coin pouch.

Ranat stood and took a swig from the almost-
empty bottle of rum. He had a couple of days before
The Library's next public day, and not a lot to do
until then.

Well, no. There was one thing he could do. Ranat
finished draining the bottle and eyed it, wondering if
he'd have a chance to get another one.

No matter, he thought. He climbed up the stairs
into the rain, looking for Gessa.

———

"*That's* your plan?" Gessa looked disgusted.

They sat in a booth in the nameless bar, leaning in close across the table, but they still needed to shout to each other over the din of voices washing back and forth around the room. Ranat wondered what was going on. He'd never seen the place so crowded before, and it seemed like most of the people knew one another.

He waited to speak as a man standing near them let out a guffaw and half-fell onto their table, almost spilling Gessa's drink before righting himself and staggering off.

"It's the—" A young woman screamed in what sounded like pain, but what looked like delight. "You want to get out of here?" he shouted across the table at Gessa.

She nodded. He followed her out, taking the bottle with him.

"It's the best thing I can come up with," he finished when they got outside.

They paused just outside the low doorway. Screams and shouts of revelry drifted through.

"It's a terrible idea, Ranat." Her voice was low, hoarse, after shouting through the cacophony of the bar.

He shrugged. "Maybe so."

"You should have left the city, back when we all thought you'd already gone."

He shrugged again, said nothing.

"It's not too late. You could still be out of Fom by dawn."

Another shrug.

Gessa sighed. "You're not going to, are you?"

"What would be the point?" he asked, voice quiet. "To live out my last days even more alone than I am now? While here, where I've spent my entire life, my name is marked for history by a crime that isn't mine?"

"Does it matter? I know you didn't kill anyone, Ranat."

"That doesn't matter," he said, then winced at his own words and took her hand in his when he saw how they'd stabbed her. "I mean," he amended, "it matters to me, sure, but what happens when you're gone? A hundred years from now, Ranat Totz will just be a murderer to anyone who bothers looking."

"I still don't understand," she muttered, not looking at him.

"You're young," he sighed.

"I'm not that young."

"Compared to me, you are. Whatever I do now, Gessa, I've only got a few years left. The name I leave behind, whatever baggage is attached to it, that's all I got."

"Damn it!" She coughed out a sob, wiped at her eyes with the backs of her hands, and looked up at him. "I still don't see why you care."

Ranat could only shrug again. "Come on," he

coaxed. "It's still early, this bottle's almost full. I'm not going anywhere yet. Back to my place?"

Gessa shook her head, pulled away from him a little. "No. Too messy. Let's go to mine."

———

The man who'd requisitioned the keg wagon's name was Alonus N'tasal, at least according to the paperwork the bar woman at The Crow's Marquis had shown him. Whatever position N'tasal held in the Church wasn't written on the form. Ranat hoped a name would be enough.

He felt so close. So close to redemption, yet so far. He just needed to connect the seal on the dead Hierophant's letter with that name, and he could prove it was N'tasal who murdered Trier N'navum, or at least by someone who worked for him.

The problem was, he'd been in The Library since the doors had opened to the public that morning, and he couldn't find the name Alonus N'tasal anywhere. He'd started with the upper vaults and worked his way down to the middling levels, but he wasn't listed in any of the indexes.

Somewhere outside The Library of Heaven and the fog that smothered it, the sun was sinking into the ocean, and Ranat was running out of time.

It didn't matter. He'd made his way to the bottom floor—sixteen vaults he'd checked, so far. Two massive rooms remained. The Heaven of Stone hoarded those who could only pay the bare minimum in Salvation Taxes, and those who'd been able to afford more, but were chronically late in their payments. The one across from it, the second-lowest of the Eighteen Heavens, the Heaven of Wood, held minor officials and the temple children who'd been plucked off the street, and the poor who'd shown exemplary service to the Church, or at least scraped together enough over the years to afford a higher level than Stone. Below lay the Void—the tomb that held the names of petty criminals and those who'd never paid. Where Ranat's name had been until his conviction, but no church officials would be down there.

And whoever N'tasal had been, he'd neither been poor nor a minor official, either. Maybe he'd used a pseudonym on the form. Ranat supposed that would've been the smart thing to do.

He needed to stand in line just to see the index of the Heaven of Wood, which itself was seven volumes of tiny printed names. He grimaced. No doubt half of them began with the letter N.

The half-hour warning chime echoed through the Vault of Wood at the same moment Ranat found the name in the enormous book. The page had not yet been reprinted, and N'tasal's name had been squeezed into the margin, the ink darker and newer than faded names around it.

Ranat hurried to the section of the vault where

N'tasal had been entered. The windows here were clear glass, but otherwise undercoated, the stark marble walls painted grey by the deepening light outside. The shelves were polished, unadorned wood.

He found the book on the second shelf up and tugged it off. The name N'tasal was easy to find. All the other names were simply listed, but N'tasal's was stamped with his crest—a buck standing under a leafless tree, over which hung a crescent moon, and denoted with a footnote. N'tasal had been cast from Flowers to Wood after a "restructuring by a Hierophant due to unbecoming behavior."

Ranat wondered what restructuring entailed. He couldn't fathom a guess, but it didn't sound good, and it had resulted in N'tasal plunging fourteen levels of Heaven.

The final bell rang. Ranat closed the book and slid it back on the shelf before shuffling out the high doors of The Library with the other common citizens, cradling the pouch with the wax fragments under his coat.

His mind raced. N'tasal arranged the meeting with Trier N'navum and requisitioned the wagon that had dumped the Hierophant's body, which still had the bloodstains to prove it. N'tasal's afterlife had also plummeted from the third Heaven to the seventeenth through the actions of an unnamed Hierophant, of which there were only five. As far as Ranat knew, only one had been in Fom.

It seemed so obvious, he wanted to burst into tears, but he didn't know if it would be enough for a nobody like Ranat to convince someone in the Church.

CHAPTER TEN

HE'D HEARD OF AN OLD LAW AS A CHILD, WHICH said if one's accuser was a member of the Church hierarchy, one could demand to face them. Peasants and foreigners had no such added responsibility, but it was only right that the clergy was held to a higher standard.

He couldn't remember where he'd heard it. Vineyard talk. Indentured servants discussing all the ways that their lives were better than their masters because at least peasants didn't need to bear the weight of responsibility. Ranat had always seen it as accepting their lot.

He also didn't know whether it was a real law or just a rumor based on a misunderstood, half-overheard one that really existed. Chatter that had spread like fire through the servant's dorms because some peasant wanted to sound like he knew what he was talking about. He'd always assumed most of what he'd learned as a child from the other indentured servants was the latter.

Well, he was about to find out.

He'd thought about going to say goodbye to Gessa one last time, but decided against it. He'd had enough of last times and final goodbyes. Anyway, he had a feeling it would just make it harder on her. Harder on them both.

He started toward the local constabulary to turn himself in but decided against that, too. It would be too easy for them to shuffle him off and forget about him, and the old oiled satchel of papers and wax fragments he clutched with both hands.

It drizzled as he hiked up the winding road that led to the top of Cathedral Hill. The Library wasn't open to the masses today, so foot traffic was light. A few of the Grace's Guard marched to and from their posts, and a steady, unhurried stream of carriages trundled, windows blocked by curtains, camels dripping rain in rivulets from their matted hair. The guards eyed Ranat when they noticed him, but nothing more.

Wise Hall clawed itself into the sky with long thin arms of white marble minarets. Beneath those, bronze domes bubbled, held aloft by polished pillars of veined marble and granite.

Ranat hesitated ten paces in front of the ancient,

worn stairs. The doors were molded from iron, thirty-hands tall and gaping open, ready to swallow him. Grace's Guard stood to either side, watching, fondling the handles of their long, curved, ceramic knives.

He approached the doors and stopped in front of the two guards.

They continued to watch, but said nothing.

Ranat cleared his throat. He'd made a conscious decision to leave his last bottle of rum at home; it had been mostly empty, anyway. Now, though, his throat was dry, and he wished he'd brought it. Now that he was here, it didn't seem like having a bottle with him would make much of a difference.

"I am," he said, trying to keep his voice even, "convicted of murdering the Hierophant, Trier N'navum."

It took a moment to sink in, but when it did, both guards' eyes grew wide. The one on the right reached out and grabbed Ranat by the arm as if the old man might decide to turn and run away. Ranat didn't resist.

"He's due for the Pit," the one that had grabbed him said.

"What, you're just going to leave your post and haul him there yourself?"

"Well, no. Alright, then." He turned to his companion. "You wait here with him while I report this."

The other frowned. "*You* wait here."

Four more guards approached from the other side of the complex, where they'd been walking when they saw something transpiring in front of the Hall.

"Sir," the first guard said to the leader of the newcomers, a dour middle-aged woman who wore an eight-pointed sun emblem in the collar of her white coat. "We caught the Hierophant's murderer, sir."

The officer was thin and tired-looking. Her hood was down, her thin black hair streaked with grey and flattened with rain. Her narrow, blunt nose dripped. "Caught? Looks like he's turned himself in." She eyed Ranat, suspicious.

"Well, regardless, we have him here. Request a replacement so I can deliver him to the Pit personally, sir."

"I demand to face my accuser," Ranat said, quiet but firm.

"What?" The officer turned back to Ranat.

The first guard, still clinging to Ranat's arm, barked a cruel laugh. "Demand? You murdering piece of ..." He trailed off under the glower of his officer.

"I demand to face my accuser," Ranat said again, louder. "As is my right, if my accuser is a member of the Hierarchy."

The guard gripped his arm tighter and shook him. "What? You think you're a lawyer? You—"

"No," the officer interrupted. "It doesn't matter who he thinks he is. He's right."

"But sir, no one ever actually—"

"Just because no one ever claims the Right of the Accused doesn't mean that the right doesn't exist."

"Um. Yes, sir." The guard seemed to conclude he wasn't in a winning position.

Learn to pick your battles, Ranat wanted to tell him, but he kept his mouth shut.

"Take this man to one of the interview rooms beneath the Hall. Feed him if he's hungry. I'll go see if I can find out who lay the charges. If it's not one of the Hierarchy, you can take him to the Pit."

"Yes, sir. Um. Does that mean someone is filling my post?"

She grunted and gestured to one of the waiting squad. "Ovin, take this man's position until he returns."

————

A surge of fear gripped Ranat when he'd heard the words "interview room" and "under the palace" in the same sentence, but no torture devices awaited him. Just a smallish, rectangular room with high windows barred with iron, a narrow table and ten chairs with thin cushions around it—four on either side and one on each end. The floor was simple white tile, the walls polished granite, unadorned except for the hooded glow lamps that hung in each corner.

They brought him food: black bread, oily broth,

and a little shapeless lump of pale, flavorless cheese. He asked for something to drink, but they only brought water.

They left him alone, but he knew the door was locked, and there'd be at least one guard outside. Probably two.

After what felt like a long time, the door clacked open. Ranat stood, heart pumping, but it was a different woman who walked in, with two armed men in tow. She might have been as old as him, but aged with infinite more grace. Her face was still smooth, her auburn hair salted with silver, hanging in waves just past her shoulders. She wore robes of red and white that whispered as they brushed the floor: a magistrate's robes.

He hesitated. "N'tasal?"

The woman smiled and arched her eyebrows as she took a seat at the end of the table. The guards stood behind her, eyes trained on Ranat, who'd settled into the chair at the opposite end.

"No." Her voice was deeper than Ranat had expected. "But I find it interesting that you know the name of the man who first brought the charge of murder against you."

He shrugged at her. She looked amused at the impropriety but waited for him to speak.

"I know my right. I want to see my accuser."

She smiled. "And I want to know how a beggar from the Lip, who's never paid his Salvation Taxes, came to know so much about obscure Church law. But we often don't get what we want, do we? Regardless," she continued, interrupting Ranat, who was about to object, "You will be granted your right. In time. It may, however, help your cause if we know the reason for your demand."

"Are you the Grace?" Ranat changed the subject suddenly.

The woman's laughter was genuine. A feminine rumble filled the room. "No, that I am not. Just a magistrate, here to observe the unfolding of Heaven's Laws."

Ranat nodded. "If my accuser is Alonus N'tasal, then that's one more piece of evidence that he's the murderer. Or, at least, the orchestrator of the murder. I doubt he was the one that did the stabbing."

"One *more* piece of evidence? So you say there's more? Because, I must say, though I hold no love for N'tasal, whom I know, your first piece of evidence is quite circumstantial."

Ranat reached into the satchel and pulled out the letter and shards of wax. "I found this on the Hierophant. There's enough left of the seal that you can tell it's N'tasal's. I didn't kill him. I just ..." He trailed off.

The magistrate arched an eyebrow. "Just looted the body?" She picked up the letter.

As she read, Ranat continued. "At the club mentioned in that letter—The Crow's Marquis—N'tasal signed a requisition so his goons could take their keg wagon to dump the body near the Lip. Send someone to check—the bloodstains in the back of the wagon and the paperwork are still there."

The woman had moved on from the letter to examine the fragments of wax and peered up. "Is that so?"

Ranat felt triumph build. "It is. He signed the requisition himself. All the dates line up. Seems like N'tasal wasn't getting along with his boss."

At that moment, the door burst open and another man, grunting under his breath, marched into the room. He was portly and mostly bald. His shaved jowls glistened with rain. Behind him were the two men who'd first arrested Ranat what seemed like ages ago and, behind them, outside the doorway, was the officer who'd directed the guards to bring Ranat to the interview room.

"What the hell is this?" the new man spat, still hovering in the doorway as if he assumed this wouldn't take long enough to bother sitting down. "Who the hell is this vagabond?" he gestured toward Ranat with his head.

A mix of recognition and worry twisted the faces of the two men behind him.

"This is the man you've accused of murdering Hierophant Trier N'navum, Alonus. He's brought up some interesting points."

"Magistrate Vaylis," N'tasal turned to the woman

as if noticing her for the first time. "Why are you even talking to this murderer? He's already been convicted. Throw him in the Pit so I can get back to work. My ship leaves tomorrow. I don't have time for this." He half-turned to go.

"He has invoked the Right of the Accused."

N'tasal scoffed. "But he's already been convicted!"

"You know as well as I do, under the Right, that doesn't matter."

"Fine. Here I am." He took a step into the room and wheeled on Ranat, face and ears turning red. "You want to see your accuser? Here I am." He thrust a pudgy finger at Ranat and turned back to the magistrate. "There. Guilty."

"I would guess," Ranat said, shocking himself with the calm of his voice, "That those two men there —" he pointed at the two bodyguards standing behind N'tasal—"would be identified by the bar staff at The Crow's Marquis as the same two who requisitioned the keg wagon the night they murdered the Hierophant." He paused, looking to the magistrate. "If you were to ask, that is."

"What?" N'tasal's head was as red as Ranat's nose.

"What, indeed, Alonus," the magistrate said, her voice calm. "What do you see here on the table in front of me?"

"What are you ..." N'tasal's voice trailed away as,

for the first time, he took in the objects on the table. His bodyguards shifted behind him.

The fat Churchman pounded the table, eyes wild. His expression contorted as he looked first to Ranat, then to the magistrate. "This is a joke! This isn't evidence. None of it! This," he picked up the letter and waved it over the table. A few more bits of wax flew from it, making tiny sounds as they rained onto the tile floor. "Means nothing! All of it is meaningless. You can't take this peasant's word over mine! He's already been convicted! This—all of it is meaningless." He trailed off again, wheezing.

"I think," she observed, "by the way you're repeating yourself, you believe anything but." She gestured toward the hallway, where the officer from the front of the Palace still hovered. "Excuse me, sir. I don't know your name."

"Mallin, Magistrate." The woman gave a little bow. "Captain Mallin."

"Captain, please have your men arrest these three. Hold them in the cells until a trial can be set."

"Yes, Magistrate."

N'tasal's two guards had broken to flee with the magistrate's words, but judging from the scuffling sounds in the hallway, hadn't made it far. N'tasal himself still stood in the same spot, sputtering indignation.

Magistrate Vaylis turned to him again and sighed.

"Oh, Alonus. It seems the Heaven of Wood was not yet low enough for you."

With that, Captain Mallin took him away.

The magistrate turned back to Ranat, who'd sat watching the spectacle unfold with no small amount of amusement.

"There is still the matter of your conviction." Her eyes were sad.

Ranat nodded. A lump formed in his throat, and his mirth fled.

"You seem to know enough of Church law to make you a noble man indeed for returning here with the truth."

He shrugged and clasped his suddenly shaking hands in front of him.

"It is beyond even the Grace's power to overturn a sentence. You must understand, the Church is infallible. It must always remain thus."

Ranat only trusted himself to give a tiny nod. Even knowing what would happen, it was hard to watch all the little stars of hope wink out, one by one, in his mind.

"You will, of course, be spared the Pit."

Ranat blinked the tears from his eyes and nodded, focused on the table in front of him.

Magistrate Vaylis chewed her lip a moment before continuing. Ranat glanced up and thought he saw a tear in her eye as well, but maybe it was just a reflection because when he looked again, it was gone.

"You will be held in Wise Hall until the end of N'tasal's trial, in which he will be found guilty if the things you have told me are true. At that time, you will be hung. Privately. No conviction will be read aloud. Just your name, which will then be written into the Heaven of Light as a martyr."

Ranat nodded again. he wiped his face and forced a smile.

"I'm sorry I cannot do more for you, Ranat Totz."

He pulled his eyes from the grain of the table and looked up at the magistrate. "You did more than I expected you'd do, I guess."

The smile she gave him was kind. "The Heaven of Light awaits you, Ranat Totz. Not even I can say as much."

He laughed. A heartfelt laugh he wasn't expecting. It burst from him and seemed to lift away the heavy weight of his life. "Yeah. Maybe. That's not was I was talking about, though. You gave me my name back—attached something to it that makes it worth leaving behind. Funny, I never thought about how much that mattered until it got taken away."

Magistrate Vaylis smiled again. "The world will be at a loss without you, Ranat Totz. You are a wise man."

Ranat smiled, showing the gap of his missing teeth, and blushed at the compliment, but all he said was, "No. No, I'm not. But thanks."

Dear Reader,

We hope you enjoyed reading *Within A Name*. Please take a moment to leave a review, even if it's a short one. Your opinion is important to us.

Discover more books by R.A. Fisher at

https://www.nextchapter.pub/authors/ra-fisher.

Best regards,

R.A. Fisher and the Next Chapter Team

You might also like:

The Swordswoman
by Malcolm Archibald

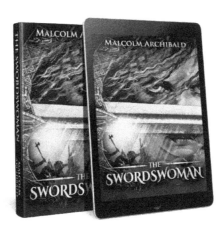

To read the first chapter for free go to:
https://www.nextchapter.pub/books/the-
swordswoman-scottish-historical-fantasy

Within A Name
ISBN: 978-4-86747-803-5
Large Print

Published by
Next Chapter
1-60-20 Minami-Otsuka
170-0005 Toshima-Ku, Tokyo
+818035793528

26th May 2021

CPSIA information can be obtained
at www.ICGtesting.com
Printed in the USA
BVHW032024140621
609528BV00007B/1248

9 784867 478035